"So who are you working for?"

She seemed casual, yet he couldn't see her eyes behind those protective shades.

"Nobody you know." And he could have sworn he saw her relax, subtly—but then, with her, how could he be sure?

He watched her finish off the skewered meat and then carefully lick the stick clean of barbecue sauce. Watched the ways her lips curved with sensual pleasure, and her little pink tongue slipped tantalizingly between them to lap every possible morsel from the skewer. When he realized hungry juices were pooling at the back of his own throat, he tore his eyes away from her and tackled his own plate.

"So...let me get this straight. You're a private investigator, hired by someone I don't know. So what is it, exactly, you want with me?"

He pointed with his fork at the card she'd left lying on the table. "If you read that, it says I specialize in finding people." He paused, took another bite. "I've been hired to find someone... and I believe that person is you."

Dear Reader,

If you've read my books before, you may have noticed a certain continuing theme. The romance is always first, of course, and then the suspense…but at the bottom of it all, what my books are really about is *family*. It isn't hard to figure out why. My own family is so precious to me and has played such an important part in shaping who I am.

When it comes to family, as Kincaid might say, we don't get to choose the hand we're dealt. But for better or worse, our families make us who we are.

And so we come to the last chapter in the series THE TAKEN. Need I tell you this is the book in which Cory's shattered family is finally reunited? I hope you've enjoyed this series as much as I've enjoyed writing it and sharing my deep and abiding love of family with you.

With warmest wishes,

Kathleen Creighton

KATHLEEN CREIGHTON

Kincaid's Dangerous Game

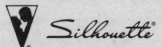

Romantic

SUSPENSE

SILHOUETTE BOOKS

ISBN-13: 978-0-373-27633-2

KINCAID'S DANGEROUS GAME

Recycling programs
for this product may
not exist in your area.

Visit Silhouette Books at www.eHarlequin.com

Printed in U.S.A.

KATHLEEN CREIGHTON

has roots deep in the California soil but has relocated to South Carolina. As a child, she enjoyed listening to old timers' tales, and her fascination with the past only deepened as she grew older. Today, she says she is interested in everything—art, music, gardening, zoology, anthropology and history, but people are at the top of her list. She also has a lifelong passion for writing, and now combines her two loves in romance novels.

For my family,
near and far;
I love you,
eccentricities, skeletons and all.

Prologue

Part 1
In a house on the shores of a small lake, somewhere in South Carolina

"Pounding…that's always the first thing. Someone— my father—is banging on the door. Banging…pounding…with his fists, feet, I don't know. Trying to break it down."

"And where are *you*?"

"I'm in a bedroom, I think. I don't remember which one. I have the little ones with me. It's my job to look after them when my father is having one of his…spells. I have to keep them out of his way. Keep them safe. I've taken them into the bedroom and I've locked the door. Except…I don't trust the lock, so I've wedged a chair under the handle, like my mom showed me. Only now I'm afraid…terrified even that won't be enough. I can hear the wood splintering…breaking. I know it will only take a few more blows and he'll be through. My mother is screaming…crying. I hold on to the little ones. I have my arms around them, and they're all trembling. The twins, the little girls, are sobbing and crying, 'Mama, Mama…' but the boys just cry quietly.

"I hear sirens…more sirens, getting louder and louder until it seems they're coming right into the room, and there's lots of people shouting. Then all of a sudden the pounding stops. There's a moment—several minutes—when all I hear is the little ones whimpering…and then, there's a loud bang, so loud we all jump. We hold each other tighter, and there's another bang, and then there's just confusion—voices shouting…footsteps running…glass breaking…the little ones crying… and I think I might be crying, too."

Cory discovered he *was* crying, but he also knew it was all right. *He* was all right. Sam, his wife, was holding him tightly, cradling his head against her breasts, and her hands were gentle as they wiped the tears from his face.

"I'm going to find them, Sam. My brothers and sisters. I have to find them."

Samantha felt warm moisture seep between her lashes. "Of course you do." She lifted her head and took her husband's face between her hands and smiled fiercely at him through her tears. "We'll find them together, Pearse," she whispered. "We'll find them. I promise you we will."

Part 2
In a diner in a small town in the Texas Hill Country

"I never thought it would happen," Cory said to Holt Kincaid over steak and eggs at the diner. "Not to Tony. He's always been…well, let's just say, he's somewhat of a lady's man. I didn't think he'd ever find…"

"The *one?*" Holt lifted one eyebrow. "Who's to say there's a *one* for everybody? Maybe some people just don't have *one* to find."

"Like you, for instance?" Cory's eyes narrowed thoughtfully as he picked up his coffee cup. "What's your story, Holt? I sense there is one—probably a helluva one, too."

Holt smiled sardonically but didn't reply.

After a moment Cory said, "So. What about my other sister? You said her name's Brenna, right? Where is she and when can I meet her?"

Holt let out a breath and pushed his plate away. It was the moment he'd been dreading. "That's gonna be a problem."

"Why? What problem? You said the twins were adopted together, grew up in the same family. Surely they've stayed in touch. Brooke must know—"

"I wish that were true." Holt picked up his coffee and blew on it, stalling for time. But there was no way around it. It looked like he was going to have to be the one to break the news that would devastate the man sitting across from him. Never mind that he'd found three of his lost siblings—two brothers and now one of his sisters. The task wouldn't be complete until he'd found the last one as well.

"Mr. Pearson, I'm sorry to have to tell you, but Brenna ran away from home when she was just fourteen. Brooke hasn't seen or heard from her since." He spread his hands in utter defeat. "I have absolutely no clue where she is. Or even where to start looking."

Chapter 1

Holt Kincaid was no stranger to insomnia. He'd been afflicted with bouts of it since childhood, and had learned long ago not to fight it. Consequently, he'd grown accustomed to whiling away the long late-night or early-morning hours catching up on paperwork, going over notes from whatever case he was working on, knowing that what he didn't pursue would come to him on its own, eventually.

Not this time.

The only case he was working at the moment—the only one that mattered, anyway—was at a dead stand-still. The paperwork had been done. He'd been over his notes a hundred times. There was nothing more to be gleaned from them.

Over the course of his career as a private investigator specializing in missing persons cases—the cold ones in particular—he'd had to admit defeat only once. That one failure was the case responsible for a lot of the insomnia he'd suffered for most of his life, and the idea that he might have to add this one to the roster of his regrets weighed heavily on his mind. Sleep wouldn't come to him this night, no matter how coyly he played her flirting game.

Laurel Canyon was quiet now. There'd been sirens earlier, prompting him, as a longtime resident, to pause and sniff the air for the smell of smoke. But the cause this time—a traffic-stopping fender bender on the boulevard—had been cleared up hours ago. An onshore breeze rustled the leaves of the giant eucalyptus trees that soared above his deck, but in a friendly way, last week's Santa Anas being only a bad memory now. Late-October rains had laid the threat of brush fires low for the time being.

Holt had come to be a resident of the notorious Santa Monica Mountain community by happenstance rather than choice, but over the years it had grown on him. He'd found it suited him, with its shady past, the steep and narrow winding dead-end streets and pervasive aura of mystery. The huge old eucalyptus trees and rickety stairways and ivy-covered walls guarded its secrets well. As he guarded his own.

He'd also come to embrace the canyon's laid-back, live-and-let-live attitude, a holdover from the sixties when it had been the center of L.A.'s rock music scene. Now as then, in Laurel Canyon the expression "goin' with the flow" wasn't just a hippie slogan, but a way of life.

It had become his way of life: Go with the flow… don't get emotionally involved…go about your business and don't waste energy railing against things beyond your control.

Yeah. That was my mistake with this case. I got too close. Made it personal.

As with the first and still his greatest failure, he'd let himself get too fogged in by emotions to see where the answers lay hidden.

Face it, Kincaid. Maybe there just aren't any answers. Not in this life, anyway.

Unbidden, as if a stubborn imp in his subconsciousness had again touched Replay, the case and the events of the past year unfolded slowly in his mind, playing out against the murmur of breezes through eucalyptus trees and the intermittent *shush* of a passing car.

He'd taken on Cory Pearson's case for two good reasons: First, because it presented a new kind of challenge. Typically, he'd be searching for a birth parent, a child given up for adoption, an abducted child long ago given up for dead by everyone except loved ones still praying for answers. But this was a man searching for four younger brothers and sisters. The children had been taken from him when they were very young by a well-meaning social services agency after their Vietnam vet father had shot his wife and then himself during a violent episode of PTSD. The four younger ones had been adopted by two different families while the oldest brother fought his way through a dismal series of foster homes and juvenile detention facilities, only to be denied access to his siblings' whereabouts when he finally reached adulthood.

A sad story, for sure, but one to which Holt had felt confident he could give a happy ending. These kids had vanished into the *system*. Systems kept records. And Holt was very good at getting old systems and old records to give up their secrets. That was his second reason for taking on the case of Cory Pearson's lost siblings: He'd expected success.

Holt didn't take on hopeless cases. He already had one of those, and it was more than enough.

Things had gone about as expected, at first. After months of tedious detective work, he'd finally gotten a line on the oldest boy, now working as a homicide detective in Portland, Oregon. The timing hadn't been great. Cory had dropped into his brother's life in the middle of a case involving a serial killer and had very nearly been mistaken for the killer himself. Thanks to a drop-dead gorgeous blond psychic who'd been helping out with the investigation, everything had turned out fine in the end, and the psychic—or empath, as she preferred to call herself—had recently become Cory Pearson's sister-in-law.

Cory's reunion with one brother was followed immediately, and without any further help from Holt, by the second. Finding his younger brother paralyzed as a result of a climbing accident, Cory'd been determined to bring him back to the life and the woman he'd loved and left. After epic battles with a wild river and a deranged killer, he and his wife, Sam, had been successful.

Two down, Holt had thought then. Two to go.

It hadn't been a piece of cake, but eventually he'd tracked down one of the twin girls. And again, his timing had been lousy—or, he supposed, depending on how you looked at it, fortuitous. He'd arrived in the woman's Texas Hill Country town to check her out only to find his client's baby sister had just been arraigned on charges of murdering her ex-husband—with the aid of a pet cougar, no less. Since both Cory and Sam had been on assignment and unreachable, Holt had called on Cory's best friend, a well-known part-Native American photojournalist named Tony Whitehall.

That had all worked out okay, too—again, depending on how you looked at it, since former confirmed bachelor Tony now appeared about to become his best buddy's brother-in-law, stepdad to a nine-year-old kid and co-caretaker of one helluva big kitty cat.

Holt had been riding pretty high that day, thinking he had the case as good as sewed up, since finding one sister meant finding both, right? Then the news had come down on him like a ton of bricks: Brenna Fallon had run away from home at the age of fourteen, and hadn't been heard from since. Her sister Brooke didn't know whether she was alive or dead. Holt didn't like remembering how he'd felt hearing that…the cold knot in his stomach, the sense of utter helplessness. This kid—though she'd be a woman in her thirties now—wasn't in any system. She'd gone completely off the radar. She could be anywhere. Or nowhere. She could very well be dead, or as good as.

He hadn't given up, though, even then. Giving up wasn't Holt's style. In the past two months he'd called in every marker, every favor he had coming and then some, and as a result had had people combing through cold case files and unclaimed Jane Doe remains in virtually every state in the union, plus Canada and Mexico. He'd personally checked out more bodies of young women dead way before their time than he'd ever expected to see in his lifetime, and armed with DNA samples from Brooke, had eliminated every one of them. Which was good news, he supposed.

But it still didn't give him answers. And three out of four wasn't going to cut it. He didn't think for one minute Cory Pearson would be content to have found three out of four of his siblings. The one he hadn't found was going to haunt him forever.

Nobody knew better than Holt Kincaid what that felt like.

He rubbed a hand over his burning eyes and turned away from the window, and from the mesmerizing sway of eucalyptus branches. Sinking onto the couch, he reached for the remote, thumbed it off Mute and began to click his way through ESPN's late-night offerings, rejecting an old George Foreman fight, some pro billiards and a NASCAR documentary before settling on a Texas Hold 'em poker tournament. Maybe, he thought, if he could get into the strategy of the game it would take his mind off the damn case.

He'd watched enough poker to know this wasn't a current tournament, more likely one from a few years back. He was familiar with some of the players, particularly the more colorful ones. Others, not so much. The commentators seemed to be excited by this event because of the fact that a woman had made it to the final table, something that evidently had been almost unprecedented back then. It didn't hurt any that the woman in question was young, blond and cute, either. Billie Farrell, her name was, and Holt thought he'd probably seen her play before. Anyway, she looked familiar to him.

Damn, but she looks familiar...

He felt an odd prickling on the back of his neck. Leaning closer, he stared intently at the TV screen, impatient with the camera when it cut to one of the other players at the table, tapping his fingers on the remote until it came back to the one face he wanted to see.

She was wearing dark glasses, as so many of the players did, to hide their eyes and not give anything away to steely-eyed opponents. She had short, tousled blond hair, cut in layers, not quite straight, not really curly, either. An intriguingly shaped mouth and delicately pointed chin, like a child's.

He really needed to see her eyes.

Take off your glasses, dammit.

He got up abruptly and crossed to the dining room table that served as his desk, half a foot deep now in manila file folders and stacks of papers he hadn't gotten around to putting in files yet. Nevertheless, he didn't have any trouble finding the one he wanted. He carried it back to the couch, sat, opened the file and took out a photograph. It was a picture of a fourteen-year-old girl, computer-aged twenty years. He didn't look at the photograph—he didn't have to, because it was etched in his memory—but simply held it while he stared at the face of the poker player known as Billie Farrell.

He wasn't conscious of feeling anything, not shock or excitement or anything in particular. Didn't realize until he fumbled around for his cell phone and had to try to punch the buttons that his hands were shaking.

It took him a couple of attempts, but he got the one he wanted. Listened to it ring somewhere in the Texas Hill Country while he stared at the TV screen with hot, narrowed eyes. When an answering machine picked up, he disconnected, then dialed the number again. This time a man's voice answered. Swearing.

"Okay, this better be an announcement of the Second Coming, or else I just won the Publishers Clearing House sweepstakes. Which is it?"

"Tony. It's me, Holt."

"Dude. D'you know what time it is?"

"Yeah. Listen, is Brooke there?"

"Of course she's here. She's asleep, what did you expect? At least, she was—" There was a sharp intake of breath. "Wait. It's Brenna, right? God, don't tell me. You found her? Is she—she's not—hey, Brooke. Baby, wake up. It's Holt. He's found—"

"Maybe," Holt interrupted. "I don't know. I need Brooke—"

"I'm here." Brooke's voice was breathy with sleep, and shaky.

"Okay." Holt took a breath. Told himself to be calm. "I need you to turn on your television. ESPN. Okay?"

"Okay." Her voice was hushed but alert. She'd been married to a deputy sheriff once upon a time, so Holt figured maybe getting phone calls in the middle of the night wasn't all that unusual for her.

"I don't know which channel," he told her. "Just keep clicking until you find the poker tournament."

After a long pause, she muttered, "Okay, got it."

"Watch for her—the woman player. Okay, there she is. Tell me if—"

He didn't get the rest of it out. There was a gasp, and then a whispered, "Oh, God."

He felt himself go still, and yet inside he was vibrating like a plucked guitar string. "Is it her? Is it Brenna?"

He heard a sniff, and when she spoke in a muffled voice he knew Brooke was crying. "Oh, God, I don't know. It could be, but she was just a little girl when she… It's been so long. I'm not *sure.* I can't see her eyes! If I could just see her eyes…" And then, angrily, "Why doesn't she take off the damn *glasses!*"

Holt held the phone and listened to soft scufflings and some masculine murmurs of comfort while he waited, eyes closed, heart hammering. After a moment Tony's voice came again, gruff with emotion.

"Hey, man, I'm sorry. She can't tell for sure. It's been what—eighteen years? She says it might be her. But you're gonna go check her out, right?"

"Yeah," Holt said, "I'm gonna go check her out." He picked up the remote and clicked off the set.

An hour later he was in his car on I-15, heading east toward the rising sun and the bright lights of Las Vegas.

He hit the jackpot right off the bat. The casino manager at the Rio was new, but Holt found a couple of dealers who'd been around awhile, and had actually worked the poker tournament he'd been watching on ESPN reruns.

Although, even if they hadn't, they would have remembered Billie Farrell.

"Sure, I remember her. Cute kid. Pretty good poker player, too," Jimmy Nguyn said as he lit up a cigarette and politely blew the smoke over his shoulder, away from Holt and the other dealer. Jimmy was a guy in his late thirties with a Vietnamese name and an American-size body—five-eleven or so and hefty. He had a card-sharp's hands, though—big and long boned, with nimble, tapered fingers. He wore a pencil-thin moustache and his hair slicked down and looked like something out of a 1930s gangster flick.

The other dealer snorted and moved upwind of the smoker. She was a tall, angular woman with sun-damaged skin and long blond hair she wore pulled up in an off-center ponytail. She'd told Holt her name was Cricket. Now she popped a piece of chewing gum in her mouth, tossed the ponytail over her shoulder and said, "Come on, Jimmy, she was more than 'pretty good.'" She looked over at Holt. "She had talent, that one, plus charisma up the wazoo. That year, the one you're talking about? Came *this close* to winning a bracelet. Woulda been a big star in the circuit, if she'd stuck around."

"Stuck around?" Holt felt his stomach go hollow.

Cricket shook her head. "Quit right after that tournament you saw, didn't she, Jimmy? That's the way I remember it, anyway. I guess it was…I don't know… pretty hard for her to tough it out, after what happened."

"What did happen?" Holt kept his voice low, hiding the despair that was rolling over him like a bank of cold Pacific fog.

She shrugged and shifted around, looking uncomfortable. "Okay, well, she had this partner…"

It was Jimmy's turn to snort. "Guy was a real scumbag." He dropped his cigarette onto the parking lot asphalt and ground it to dust under his shoe as he said musingly, "Miley Todd was his name. Never did get what a young pretty girl like that saw in him. The guy cheated and got caught," he explained to Holt. "Got himself banned from the casinos for life."

"Billie was clean, though," Cricket put in.

Jimmy lifted a shoulder. "Yeah, okay, the kid probably was clean. But there'd have been talk. There's always talk. Rumor and innuendo—you know how it is. Carries a lot of weight in this town."

"I don't think that's why she quit," the blond dealer said, quick to jump to another woman's defense. "Billie was tougher than that. Tough as nails. What made her such a good player. If she'd wanted to stay, she would have."

Jimmy held up a hand. "I'm just sayin'…"

Cricket gave him a dismissive look and focused on Holt. "All I know is, she won pretty big that night— finished in third place—and she took her money and split. That's the last the poker world saw of her."

Holt hauled in a breath. "Okay, then, thanks for your time." He couldn't turn away fast enough. It was all he could do to keep his disappointment in check, and what he wanted more than anything was to slam his fist into something and cuss until he ran out of words bad enough. To come so close. And now it looked like he was right back at square one. Well, maybe not square one, since at least he had a name and a town.

"Hey," Cricket called out to him as he was about to open the door of his car, "you asking about Billie, I'm assuming you're looking to find her, right?"

Holt turned to look back at her. "Yes, I sure am."

"Well, then, don't you want to know where she is?"

* * *

"Excuse me, miss. Could you help me out here?"

Billie gave the hose nozzle a twist to shut off the water and lifted what she hoped was a helpful smile to the customer who was standing a few feet away with a bedraggled gallon-size Michaelmas daisy in one hand and a fading sedum in the other.

She'd noticed the guy wandering up and down the aisles, first because she'd never seen him before, second because he looked a lot like Clint Eastwood. In his prime. And third, because he didn't look like the sort of person to be browsing in a nursery on a weekday morning. He was wearing slacks and a sport-type jacket, for one thing, instead of jeans and a T-shirt. He wore a dress shirt with no tie, open at the neck, which gave him a casual, rumpled look in spite of the dressy clothes. Still, he looked out of place, Billie thought. Dirty Harry in a flower shop. And she had a pretty good sense for people who seemed "off" in any way. Her survival, for a good part of her life, had depended on it.

"Sure," she said, wiping her hands on her blue cotton apron. "What can I do for you?"

He shifted the two pots up and down, like he was trying to gauge their weight.

"I'm looking for something pretty with flowers. These look a little...I don't know...tired." He'd put on a smile, but it didn't look comfortable on him. As if, Billie thought, turning on the charm wasn't something that came naturally to him.

She studied him covertly from behind her sunglasses. "You'd have better luck with annuals this time of year. We're starting to get in some cool-weather stuff now. Be more in a week or two."

"Yeah, but they die, don't they? I'm looking for something you don't have to plant new every year."

Billie shrugged and nodded toward the pots in his hands. "Well, those two you got there are perennials. They'll come back every year."

"Yeah…" He said it with a sigh and a disappointed look at the sedum. "I was hoping to find something that looks a little nicer in the pot. Actually, it's for a gift." He gave her the smile again, along with an explanation. "My sister's getting married Saturday. They've bought this house here, and it looks pretty bare to me—one of those new subdivisions south of town. I thought maybe I'd get her some plants—pretty it up a bit."

"Ah, well…fall's not a good time for perennials. Sorry." She gave the hose nozzle a twist and turned the spray onto the thirsty crepe myrtles spread out in front of her.

"Look—" The guy set the two pots down next to the crepe myrtles and dusted off his hands. "I hate to be a pain in the ass, but I'm getting kind of desperate here."

I believe that's the first truthful thing you've said to me. She didn't say that, of course. She turned off the water and laid the hose carefully aside, out of the pathway, then angled another measuring look upward as she straightened. She could almost feel the guy vibrating, he was so tense. *Mister, I hope you're not planning on playing any poker while you're in town. You'd lose your shirt.*

All her defenses were on red alert. Clearly, the guy wanted something, and she seriously doubted it was potted plants. But if her danger instincts were aroused, so was her natural curiosity—which admittedly had gotten her into trouble more than once in her life.

Who is this guy? What does he want with me?

And most important of all, and the question she really, really needed an answer to: *Who is he working for?*

Giving the man the smile he seemed to be trying so hard to win, she said, "Well, there's no need for *that.* Look, why don't you go with some kind of shrub? You can get something with some size, so it'll look impressive up there with all the other wedding presents."

"Impressive. Okay, I can live with that. So, what've you got?"

"Well, let's narrow it down a bit. First, since you said this house is in a new subdivision, I'm guessing no trees, right? So you'll need something for full sun. And heat tolerant, obviously—this *is* Las Vegas." She turned to walk along the pathway and the man fell in beside her, strolling in a relaxed sort of way, reaching out to touch a leaf as they passed. She gave him a sideways glance. "How do you feel about cactus?"

He winced and laughed, as if she'd made a joke.

"I'm serious. More and more people are going with native plants now to save water. Save the planet—you know, go green."

"So to speak," he said dryly, and she found herself smiling and meaning it.

"So to speak." She nodded, conceding the point. "So, okay, no cactus. Evergreen, or deciduous?"

"Deciduous—uh…that means they lose their leaves, right?"

She looked at him and he grinned to show her he was kidding. This time she tried not to smile back. "You seriously are not a gardener, are you? Where are you from?"

"Nope," he said amicably, "definitely not a gardener. And I live in L.A., actually."

"Really. Most people in L.A. have some kind of garden."

"Not me. Not even a houseplant." He paused, then added with a shrug, "I'm not home enough to take care of anything living. I've got eucalyptus trees and ivy, some bougainvillea—that's about it. Nature pretty much takes care of those."

He halted suddenly and pointed with a nod. "What are those? Over there—with all the flowers?"

Billie gave him a look. "Uh…roses?"

"Okay, sure, I see that now," he said, throwing her a sheepish grin before returning to stare thoughtfully at the display of rosebushes. "Can you grow roses in Las Vegas?"

"We wouldn't sell them if they wouldn't grow here," she said shortly, and got a look of apology that made her feel vaguely ashamed. Her mind was skittering around like a squirrel trying to decide whether or not to run into traffic.

The guy is attractive and charismatic as hell, and he still smells wrong. Well, actually, he smells pretty good. Whatever he's using for aftershave, it was a good choice.

She hauled in a determined breath. "Actually, roses do very well in a desert climate. Less trouble with disease. You just have to give them enough water."

"Hmm. Roses kind of go with weddings, don't they?"

"Sure. I suppose so. Yeah."

"They'd definitely be impressive," he mused.

"Yes, they would."

"And they have pretty flowers."

About then Billie realized they'd both stopped walking and were standing in the middle of the aisle smiling at each other. Really smiling. And her heart was beating faster, for no earthly reason she could imagine.

Okay, I'm not a squirrel. I know what happens to squirrels who run into traffic.

She cleared her throat and walked on with purpose, making her way quickly to the rosebushes. "Your timing is good, actually. They put out a nice fall bloom, once the weather cools. Couple more weeks, though, and we'd be pruning them back for the winter."

The customer picked up a red rosebush in a three-gallon pot, read the tag and threw her a look as he set it back down. "Well, you've saved my life, you know that?" He moved aside a pink variety—he was a guy, of course, so no pink need apply—and picked up a butter-yellow with some red blush on the petals. "You're very good at your job. You must like it." He said it casually, maybe *too* casually.

"Yes, I do," she replied carefully, and felt her skin prickle with undefined warnings.

He straightened, dusting his hands. "If you don't mind my asking, how'd you come to work in a nursery? In this town, someone with your looks…" He smiled again, but his eyes seemed a little too sharp. A little too keen. "Seems an unusual career choice."

And again she thought, This guy better never try his hand at the poker tables—with a tell like that, he'd never win a hand. "Maybe," she said evenly, "that's why I made it."

Watching his eyes, she knew he was about to fold.

"Well…okay, tell you what," he said abruptly, all business now. "How 'bout if you pick out half a dozen or so of these—the nicest ones you can find." He reached for his wallet. "Can I pay for them and leave them here until Saturday? Because I'm in a hotel, and I can't exactly…"

"Sure." Suddenly she just wanted to be rid of him. "That's fine. Just tell them at the register. Six, right? I'll put a note on them, put them back for you."

He thanked her and walked away, rapidly, like somebody who'd just remembered he had somewhere to be.

Billie watched him as far as the cash register, then turned abruptly. Angry. At herself. And shaken. The guy had folded, no question about it. So why didn't she feel like she'd won the hand?

* * *

Holt was sitting in his car with the motor running and the air-conditioning going, although it was November and not that hot for Las Vegas. But considering it was midday and he was in the middle of a treeless parking lot, he was pretty sure he'd be sweltering shortly if he turned the AC off.

He wasn't pleased with the way things had gone with Billie Farrell. Definitely not his finest hour. He'd turned on the charm—as much as he was capable of—and had gotten nowhere.

So she was wary, on her guard. He hadn't wanted to push too hard, thinking he'd be better off to leave himself someplace to go with his next try. Which was why he was sitting in the parking lot staking out the nursery, waiting for her to come out so he could follow her, see where she lived, find out where she liked to go for lunch. Figure out how he might "happen" to run into her again. Maybe this time he'd offer to buy her a drink, or even dinner.

If he could just get her someplace indoors where she'd have to take off those damn shades…

Meanwhile, what in the world was he going to do with six rosebushes? Donate them to an old folks' home? He'd have to think of something. Hell, he didn't even *know* anybody who grew roses.

When someone knocked on the window of his car about six inches from his ear, he did three things simultaneously: Ducked, swore and reached for his weapon.

Then he remembered he wasn't carrying one at the moment, that it was currently in the glove compartment of his vintage Mustang. By which time he figured if anybody had been looking to do him damage it would already be lights-out.

However, he was still swearing a blue streak when the door on the passenger side opened and Billie Farrell slipped into the seat beside him.

Chapter 2

She looked flushed and exhilarated, almost gleeful—and why shouldn't she? She aimed a look at the open front of Holt's jacket, inside which his hand was still clutching his shirt in the area over his rapidly thumping heart.

"Well, I guess that tells me one thing about you. Whoever the hell you are. You're used to packin'."

"Actually," he muttered darkly, "I'm just checking to see if I'm having a heart attack. Jeez, Billie." He slid his hand out of his jacket and ran it over his face, which had broken out in a cold sweat. "What were you thinking? If I had been *packing*, I'd have probably shot you—you know that, don't you?"

She shrugged, but behind the dark glasses her gaze

was steady, and he could almost feel the intensity of it. "Nuh-uh. If you'd been packin' I'd have seen it when you took out your wallet. See, I notice things like that. That's because I used to be in the kind of business where you need to notice things like that. But then, since you know my name, you knew that already."

Holt returned the measuring stare, his mind busy trying to gauge how much further he could reasonably hope to carry on with his charade as a horticulturally challenged out-of-town wedding guest. Or whether he should just pack it in and go with the truth.

Not being happy with either option, he decided to go with something in between. He held up a hand. "Okay, look. I recognized you. I've watched you play. I admit it—as soon as I saw you, I knew that was you, and... well—" and it was only the truth, wasn't it? "—I wanted to meet you."

"It's been years since I played poker." Although she looked away and her voice was quiet, she didn't relax one iota.

And although he nodded and gave her a rueful smile, he didn't, either. "I watch old poker tour reruns on television when I can't sleep. The game fascinates me. I know it's got to be more about skill than just dumb luck, because the same people always seem to make it to the final table."

Her eyes came back to him, her lips curved in a half smile. "Oh, believe me, luck still has a whole lot to do with it." Her head tilted, and the dark lenses taunted him.

"Please tell me you're not planning on trying your hand at the game while you're in town."

"Well, actually…"

"Oh, lord." She faced front again and hissed out a sigh.

"What? Why not?" He straightened, genuinely affronted.

She laughed without sound. "Why not? Well, okay, go ahead, if you don't mind losing. Just do yourself a favor, stay away from the high-stakes tables."

"What makes you so sure I'd lose? I'll have you know I do pretty well at online poker."

"Sure you do, because nobody can see your face."

"What's that supposed to mean?" he demanded.

"You really want to know?"

"Yeah," he said, and meant it.

They were bantering, he realized, though there was nothing light or easy about it. The tension in the car was almost tangible, like a low-pitched humming, but something felt along the skin rather than heard through the ears. He had the impression she was playing him, flirting with him, deliberately trying to distract him from whatever his agenda was.

But, without being able to see her eyes, of course, he couldn't be sure.

"Mister—"

"It's Holt."

"Well, Holt, you've got tells a child could read. Okay?"

"Come on."

She smiled, and this time a pair of dimples appeared unexpectedly. "Look, don't get insulted. Most people have 'em and aren't even aware they do. That's why you see so many poker players wearing hats and dark glasses."

"Is that why you do?" he asked softly.

The dimples vanished. "Like I said, I don't play the game anymore. I guess I've still got the habit." She waited a couple of beats before continuing. "Do you even have a sister?"

Holt snorted and didn't bother to answer. He listened to the shush of the air-conditioning and the throb of the idling motor and the hum of that unrelenting tension, and Billie sat there and listened along with him. Patient, he thought. Probably one of the things that had made her a success at the poker tables. Because in spite of what she'd said, he knew it was more than just luck.

He exhaled, conceding her the hand. "Okay, so you made me." He paused, then said, "I'm curious, though. How come you're here? Sitting in my car? Making conversation?"

"Why not? It's a nice car.

Then it was her turn to huff out air, too softly to be called a snort. "You're familiar with that old saying, 'Keep your friends close, and your enemies closer'?"

He jerked—another tell, he was sure, but what the hell. "I'm not your enemy."

"Well, sure, you'd say that." The almost-smile played with her lips again. "Tell you what, Holt—is that a first name or a last, by the way?"

"First. It's Holt Kincaid."

"Okay, so…Holt. Why don't I let you buy me lunch and you can tell me who you are and what you really want. And I'm willing to bet the farm it ain't rosebushes."

He laughed, then sat still and did a slow five-count inside his head. Then, still slowly, before he shifted from Park into Drive he reached up and unhooked his sunglasses from the sun visor and put them on. And heard her knowing chuckle in response.

He didn't *think* he'd let himself show the triumph he was feeling, but he was beginning to realize that with this lady, there was no such thing as a sure bet.

She directed him to an all-you-can-eat Chinese buffet place in a strip mall not far from the nursery, and since it was fast, convenient and kind to the pocketbook, Holt figured she was probably a regular there. That theory was confirmed when Billie gave a wave and a friendly greeting to the two women at the cash register—mother and daughter, by the look of them—and got smiles in return.

She breezed through the dining room, heading for a booth way in the back, one he happened to notice was turned sideways to the entrance so that neither of them would have to sit with their backs to the door. Somehow he doubted that was a coincidence.

"Is this okay?" she asked with apparent innocence. And although the lighting was low, she didn't take off those shades.

"Sure," he said, and she swept off to the buffet.

Because he didn't entirely trust her not to slip out while he was dithering between the kung pao chicken or the sweet-and-sour shrimp, Holt got himself a bowl of wonton soup and settled back in the booth where he could keep an eye on her. He watched her slip in and out among the browsing diners, adroitly avoiding reaching arms and unpredictable children, wasting little time in indecision, since she obviously knew exactly what she wanted.

And he felt an odd little flutter beneath his breastbone when it occurred to him he wasn't just watching her because she was someone he needed to keep track of. He was watching her for the sheer pleasure of it.

Okay, so she's attractive, he thought, squirming in the booth while a spoonful of wonton sat cooling halfway between the bowl and his mouth. *So what?* Given what he was pretty certain was her genetic makeup, that was no big surprise. So far, all of Cory Pearson's siblings had been exceptionally attractive people. Why should this one be any different?

And yet, she *was* different. He couldn't put his finger on what made her so, but she was. Not beautiful, and certainly not pretty—both of those adjectives seemed both too much and too little to describe her heart-shaped face and neat, compact little body. She wasn't tall and willowy, like her twin sister Brooke, and while her hair was blond and neither curly nor straight—also like Brooke's—hers was a couple of shades darker and cut in haphazard layers, and it looked like she might be in the habit of combing it with her fingers. He couldn't tell about her eyes, of course. But, maybe due to being unable to see past the shades, he'd spent quite a bit of time looking at her mouth. It fascinated him, that mouth. Her lips weren't particularly full, but exquisitely shaped, with an upward tilt at the corners. And then there were those surprising dimples. Her teeth weren't perfectly straight, which led him to surmise she'd run away from home before the mandatory teenage orthodontia had taken place. In an odd sort of way, he was glad.

What she was, he decided, was dynamic. There was just something about her that drew his gaze and held it, like a magnet.

"That all you're having?" She asked it in that breathless way she had as she slipped into the booth opposite him, carrying a plate loaded with an impossible amount of food.

"Just the first course." He stared pointedly at her heaped plate. "Is that all *you're* having?"

"Just the first course." She contemplated the assortment on her plate, then picked up her fork, stabbed a deep-fried shrimp and dunked it into a plastic cup containing sweet-and-sour sauce. "So, what are you, some kind of cop?" She popped the morsel into her mouth and regarded him steadily while she chewed.

Holt raised his eyebrows. "What makes you think that?"

"Oh, please." She forked up something with a lot of broccoli and bean sprouts. "You have cop written all over you."

He didn't know how to answer that, so he didn't, except for a little huff of unamused laughter. She was beginning to annoy the hell out of him, with this cat and mouse game she was playing.

He pushed his soup bowl aside, and instantly a very young Chinese girl was there to whisk it away and give him a shy smile in exchange. He watched her quick-step across the room while he pondered whether or not to ask Billie why she was so well acquainted with cops, since in his experience your everyday law-abiding citizen wouldn't be able to spot a cop unless he was wearing a uniform and a badge. He decided there wasn't much point in it, since he was pretty sure she'd only tell him what she wanted him to know—either that, or an outright lie.

He excused himself and went to the buffet, where he spent less time deciding on his food selections than on how he was going to handle the next round with Billie Farrell. He was beginning to suspect she might not be an easy person to handle. Maybe even impossible. He'd already concluded that asking her direct questions wasn't likely to get him anywhere. So maybe he ought to try letting her do the asking. See where that led him.

"So," he said affably as he slid back into the booth and picked up his fork, "where were we?"

"You were about to tell me you're a cop," Billie said, studying what food was left on her plate—which wasn't much.

"Was." He gave her an easy smile. "Not anymore. Haven't been for quite a while."

"Ah. Which means you're private. Am I right?" She glanced up at him and hitched one shoulder as she picked up a stick with some kind of meat skewered on it. She nibbled, then added without waiting for his reply, "Otherwise you wouldn't still have the look."

"The look…" He muttered that under his breath, then exhaled in exasperation and took one of his business cards out of his jacket pocket and handed it to her.

She glanced at it but didn't pick it up. "So. Who are you working for?" It seemed casual, the way she said it—but then, he couldn't see her eyes.

"Nobody you know." And he could have sworn he saw her relax, subtly. But then, with her, how could he be sure?

He watched her finish off the skewered meat then carefully lick the stick clean of barbecue sauce. Watched the way her lips curved with sensual pleasure, and her little pink tongue slipped tantalizingly between them to lap every possible morsel from the skewer. When he realized hungry juices were pooling at the back of his own throat, he tore his eyes away from her and tackled his own plate.

"So…let me get this straight. You're a private dick—"

"Investigator."

"Sorry—investigator, hired by somebody I don't know, and… What is it, exactly, you want with me?"

Chewing, he pointed with his fork at the card she'd left lying on the table. "If you read that, it says I specialize in finding people." He paused, took another bite. "I've been hired to find someone." He glanced up at her. "And I believe you might be able to help me."

"Hmm." She stared down at her plate while above the dark glasses her forehead puckered in what seemed to be a frown. "Why?"

"Why what? Why do I think you can help me?"

She shook her head. "Why do you—or the people you work for—want to find this person?" The dark lenses lifted and regarded him blankly. He could see twin images of himself reflected in them, which, of course, told him nothing. "There's all kinds of reasons to want to find somebody, you know."

"It's kind of complicated," Holt said, picking up his napkin and wiping his lips with it. Stalling because he hadn't decided whether it was time to put his cards on the table—and why was it everything that came into his mind seemed somehow related to poker? "But I can tell you, the people who hired me don't mean this person any harm."

"Yeah, well, there's all kinds of ways to do someone harm." She cast a quick look over her shoulder at the buffet tables, then abruptly slid out of the booth, leaving her almost-empty plate behind.

Leaving Holt to contemplate her words and complexities while he stared at her plate and a low-intensity hum of excitement vibrated through his chest. He was becoming more and more certain he'd found his client's last missing sibling, and equally certain she was never going to willingly admit to her true identity, for reasons he couldn't quite figure out. He was going to have to find another way to positively prove Billie Farrell was, in fact, Brenna Fallon.

The plate she'd left sitting on the table seemed to shimmer and grow in size as he gazed at it. For some reason the girl with the quick hands hadn't whisked it away yet, evidently being occupied elsewhere in the dining room. Billie was busy, too, heaping a salad-size plate with goodies from the dessert table. Holt threw them both a glance, then plucked the wooden barbecue skewer off of Billie's plate and wrapped it carefully in a clean paper napkin.

Billie had no idea what she was putting on her plate; the buffet table in front of her was a blur. Her heart was pounding, although she was confident nobody watching her would ever guess it.

Watching me...

Yeah. She could feel the detective's eyes on her, those keen blue eyes that wouldn't miss much. She knew she had the advantage on him, since she could read him pretty well and, unless he was a whole lot better than most of the other opponents she'd faced, he wouldn't be able to read her at all. But somehow she had to figure out how to get him to tell her more about who he was working for and exactly who they wanted him to find.

Okay, dummy, you know it has to be you they are looking for. The more important question is, why?

A week ago she'd have had to guess it was that jerk, Miley, trying to track her down. But he'd already managed to do that on his own, and besides, he'd be too cheap to hire a private dick. And even if he did somehow happen to have the money, he'd use it to get in a poker game somewhere.

Beyond that possibility, her mind refused to go.

But thinking about Miley Todd had given her an idea how to play this guy Kincaid. It was a strategy Miley had taught her way back when he was first teaching her to play poker: Start talking about herself, not a lot, just a little bit. Get her opponents relaxed and hoping for more. Then maybe they'd let their guard down and tell her what *she* wanted to know.

"So," she said in a breezy way as she slipped back into the booth, "where were we?"

"You were about to tell me whether you're going to help me find the person I'm looking for," Holt said absently, staring at her plate. "My God, are you going to eat all that?"

She focused on the mess before her and felt a wave of queasiness. Lord, was that *pudding?*

"What can I say? I have a sweet tooth." She picked up an almond cookie and nibbled on its edges while she studied him through her dark glasses. She tilted her head and let him see her dimples. "See, the thing is, how do I know if I can help you if I don't know who you're looking for?"

"A young woman," Holt said easily. "About your age, actually."

"Uh-huh…and you think she's here in Vegas?"

"I think she might be, yes."

"All right, here's the thing." She dropped the cookie

onto her plate, barely noticing that it landed in the pudding. "If I seem like I'm being a little bit cautious, it's because I've had to be. You understand? I've been in this town a long time. Nowadays, poker is pretty respectable, mainstream, but back when I first started playing, some of the people you brushed elbows with might not be the most upstanding citizens, if you know what I mean."

The detective nodded. "Like Miley Todd?"

She let go a little bubble of laughter and was grateful again for her shades. She picked up a grape and popped it into her mouth. "O—kay…so you've been checking up on me. Why am I not surprised?"

"I'm an investigator," he said with a shrug. "It's what I do." He pushed aside his plate and leaned toward her, forearms on the table. "Look, I know you and this guy, Todd, used to be partners, and that a few years back he got caught cheating and banned from the casinos."

Billie gave a huff of disdain. "He was an idiot. Card-smart, maybe, but people-stupid. A little bit of success and he started thinking he was smarter than everybody else."

"So, how did you get involved with this guy?"

She didn't move or gesture, but he could almost hear the doors slamming shut. It occurred to him that even without being able to see her eyes, he was learning to read her. "It was a long time ago. I was young—what can I say?"

He almost smiled at that, given how young she still was—a lot younger than he was, anyway. Instead, he said casually, the way he might have asked her if she liked wine, "What kind of partners were you? Professional, lovers…"

Unexpectedly, she smiled. "I'd be lying if I said I didn't see that coming."

He smiled back.

The air between them seemed to change subtly… become heavier, charged with electricity. She thought of the wild Texas thunderstorms she'd loved as a child, and realized with a shiver of fear that it was the first time in years she'd allowed herself to remember those times. She wondered why. *Why now, with this man?*

Still smiling, she hitched one shoulder. "I know how guys think. It was the first thing you thought of. But the answer is, no, we weren't lovers. Not that Miley didn't have ideas along those lines when he first met me." She picked up another grape and crunched it audibly between her teeth. "Until I told him what I'd do to him if he ever laid a hand on me."

"Ouch." He gave a pained laugh and shifted in his seat. Moments passed, and Billie could almost hear thunder rolling away in the distance. Then his gaze sharpened, focused on her again. "So…your partnership was strictly professional, then. I'm not clear on how that works in poker."

She shook her head, mentally reining herself in, sharpening her own focus. Reminding herself of her game plan. "Partnership probably isn't the right word. Miley was more like my mentor, I guess you could say.

Protector, too, sometimes. At first." She paused. "Vegas could be a rough town, back then." *Don't kid yourself, it still is.* "I'll tell you one thing, though." She sat back in the booth, as far as she could get from that plateful of sweets, having lost her appetite completely. "He was a good teacher."

He sat very still, regarding her without changing his expression, and it occurred to her that in a very short time he'd become very good at controlling those unconscious tells of his. Either that, or he'd been playing her all along. A small frisson of warning sifted coldly across the back of her neck.

"Do you ever take off those sunglasses?" he asked in the same soft, uninflected voice he'd been using to ask about her relationship with Miley.

"During a game, never," she shot back just as quietly.

"That's what this is to you…a game?"

"Sure it is. It's a lot like poker. We're both holding cards the other can't see and would really, really like to." She paused and gave him her game smile—confident, apologetic, serene. "And you know…sooner or later, one of us is going to have to call."

He expelled air in an exasperated puff, then looked over at the buffet tables, frowned and muttered, "I need some dessert," the way someone might say, "I need a drink."

"Have some of mine." Having obviously rattled him, she was enjoying herself again.

He aimed the frown at her, then at her plate. His eyebrows rose. "Is that pudding?"

"Yeah, and you're welcome to it." She slid the plate toward him, then rested her chin in the palm of her hand and watched him pick up his spoon, scoop up a bite of the stuff, frown at it, then put it in his mouth. She felt an absurd and totally unfamiliar urge to giggle.

"So…" Still frowning, he took another bite. "Who's going to call—you or me?"

"You really aren't much of a card player, are you?" She was feeling amused, relaxed, confident, sure she had the upper hand again. "If I call, you've got two choices—fold or show me your cards."

He stared at the spoon, his frown deepening. "Yeah, but you have to pay for the privilege, as I recall." His eyes lifted and shot that keen blue gaze right into hers. As if he could see through her dark glasses. As if he could see into her soul.

Cold fingers took another walk across the back of her neck. A reminder that with this guy she couldn't afford to let her guard down, not even for a moment.

"This isn't poker," she snapped, no longer amused, relaxed or confident. "And let's quit the poker analogies, which I could think of a whole lot more of, but what's the point? Here's the deal—I don't give a damn who you're looking for or who you're working for, and if you don't want to tell me, that's okay with me. Now—" she slid out of the booth and stood up "—are we done here?"

"The person I work for," Holt said, pushing aside the dessert plate and reaching for his wallet, "hired me to find his two younger brothers and twin sisters. So far, I've found the brothers and one of the twins." He took out some bills and laid them on the table, then looked up at Billie. "That twin's name is Brooke Fallon. Her sister's name is Brenna. She ran away from home when she was fourteen." He tucked his wallet away again and waited.

The silence at the table was profound, but inside Billie's head was the tumultuous crashing sound of her world falling apart.

"So?" she said, and could not feel her lips move. She was vaguely surprised to find she was sitting down again.

"So, I thought you might be my client's missing baby sister," he said softly, as he slid out of the booth. "And if you were, I thought you might be interested to know you've got a family that's looking for you."

She shook her head…pursed her lips, stiff though they were. "Sorry. Not me. Don't know her."

"Hmm," Holt said, gazing down at her, "if that's true, I'll be really disappointed. I guess I'll have to wait for the DNA to tell me whether I have to keep looking for Brenna Fallon, or whether I've already found her."

"Wait." A breath gusted from her lungs. She reached out and snagged his jacket sleeve as he turned away. "What are you talking about? I'm not giving you my DNA. You're not a cop, you can't—"

His smile was gentle. "Oh, but you've already given me what I need." He reached inside his jacket and pulled out what appeared to be a folded paper napkin. Unfolded it and showed her what was inside.

Only years of practice at keeping her face and body

under strictest control prevented her from blowing it completely. She stared at the thin wooden stick nestled in white paper in complete silence, and her mind was empty of thought. But somewhere in the primal recesses of her consciousness, a terrified child was screaming—*Run.*

Chapter 3

Still smiling, Holt tucked the folded napkin and its contents away in his inside jacket pocket. The smile was only for show. He didn't have any idea whether DNA could be recovered from the wooden skewer, and he didn't know whether Billie would see through his bluff. Or, as she would no doubt put it, *call* him on it.

Waiting at the cash register for the mother-daughter duo to process his credit card, with his peripheral vision he could see her still sitting just as he'd left her, staring straight ahead, apparently at nothing. He wondered what in the hell she was going to do now. Was she really going to let him just walk away? He was her ride back to the garden shop, of course, but it wasn't that far if she decided she'd rather walk.

What was going through her mind right now?

He wished now that he'd taken a little more time to study her playing style before rushing off to Vegas to meet her. He had no clue how this woman's mind worked.

He signed the receipt, tucked it and his credit card in his wallet and returned the wallet to his pocket, then turned to check once more on his erstwhile lunch companion. His heart did a skip and a stumble when he saw that the booth where she'd been sitting was now empty.

Swearing, he slammed through the double doors and half ran to the parking lot. She wasn't there. Since there was no way she could have gone farther in the time available, he reversed course and got to the restaurant's foyer just in time to meet her as she came out of the restroom, drying her hands on her jeans and looking completely unperturbed.

"Ah, there you are," Holt said, hoping she wouldn't pick up on the fact that his heart was pounding and he was breathing like a marathon runner. "I was about to go off without you."

"Yeah, right," she said as she walked past him and pushed through the double doors. She was smiling that damn little half-smile of hers, the one that made her seem ancient and all-knowing.

About halfway to the car she threw him a sideways glance and said in an amused tone, "Do you really think you can get DNA from a wooden stick?"

"I don't know," Holt replied. "I guess I'm about to find out."

She laughed. It was a low, husky sound, but like a shrilling alarm clock, it awoke the sensual awareness of her that had been dozing just below the levels of his consciousness. His skin shivered with it, a pleasurable sensation he tried without success to deny.

Determined to ignore it, he unlocked her side of the car and went around to do the same to his, since his restored 1965 Mustang didn't come equipped with power door-locks. He slid into his seat as she did hers, and from the corner of his eye he saw her run her hands appreciatively over the black leather upholstery. He was suddenly acutely aware of the warmth of the leather seat on his backside. Although it was comfortably cool outside, the air in the car seemed too thick to breathe.

He got the engine turned on and the air-conditioning going full blast, and as he was waiting for it to take effect, she said in that same throaty voice, "I really do like your car, by the way."

"Thanks." Good God, what now? Was she actually flirting with him?

"Did you restore it yourself?"

"No. I got it from a grateful client." He backed out of the parking place, then abruptly shifted gears and pulled back into it. "Tell me something," he said as he slapped the gearshift into Neutral. "Why should you be afraid of the DNA result anyway?"

"Who says I'm afraid?"

"It's not like you're wanted by the police," he went on, "or a suspect in a crime. All this is, is a family that's trying to find their missing sister."

Sister. Sistersistersister… Thank God he couldn't see inside her mind, see that word pulsing there like the gaudiest neon on the Vegas Strip. Thank God for the years of training that would keep him from knowing the pain she felt with every starburst.

"Yeah, well," she said, hating the gravel in her voice, "see, that's the thing. I'm nobody's sister. Okay?" *Don't deserve to be. Don't you understand? I lost that right a long time ago.*

"Pity," Holt said softly, putting the Mustang once more into reverse. "These are some nice people. You couldn't ask for a better family to be a part of."

Yeah, right, Billie thought, and it was all she could do to keep from erupting in derisive laughter. *Nice* didn't come anywhere close to describing the brother she remembered.

Then…something he'd said. Something that had been blasted out of her head at the time by the sound of that name: *Brooke Fallon.* But…she remembered now. He'd said *brothers.* Plural. But how could that be? She only had *one* brother.

"So, tell me about 'em," she said, concentrating everything she had on keeping her tone light, making her interest seem only casual. Inside her head was a cacophony of thoughts, a jabbering madhouse of incomprehension and confusion, a babel of questions she couldn't ask without giving herself away.

"Why should you want to know?" He tossed her a look as he headed out of the parking lot. "If you're not, as you say, the person I'm looking for, it's got nothing to do with you."

Panic seized her. It was only a few short blocks to the garden center; he'd be dropping her off in a minute or two. But she had to know. *She had to know.*

She could feel herself beginning to tremble inside. How much longer could she keep him from noticing?

She shrugged with elaborate unconcern. "Hey, it sounds like an interesting story, okay?" Paused at a traffic light, he looked over at her again, smiling sardonically. She gave him back her most winning smile. "I'd really like to hear it."

Holt felt a quickening, a swift surge of exultation. He'd never been fishing in his life, but he imagined this must be what a fisherman experienced when he felt that unmistakable tugging on his line. "It's kind of a long story," he said with doubt in his voice. "Don't you have to get back to work?"

There was a moment of absolute silence, yet he could hear her sigh of frustration like a faint breath, hear the crackle of tension in her muscles and joints like the rustling of fabric on skin. He wondered if it was because he couldn't read her the usual way, with his eyes, that he seemed to be developing the ability to pick up on her with his other senses.

The garden center loomed ahead. Holt slowed, turned into the parking lot. He pulled into the first empty space he came to and stopped, leaving the motor running, then looked over at Billie. She was sitting motionless, facing forward, and from her profile he could see behind her glasses, for once. Her eyes were closed. For some reason that jolted him, and he saw her in a way he hadn't been able to up till now.

Vulnerable.

"Yeah. Okay, sure." She let out a careful breath and gave him a thin, empty smile—no dimples, this time. "Listen, thanks for lunch." She opened the door, slid her legs out, then looked back at him. "And good luck finding her—the person you're looking for." She got out of the car.

He was in a quandary, letting her go. He wondered if this was what a fisherman would call letting the fish "run." If it was, he decided he didn't have the nerve for it. He had her hooked, he was sure of it. Had her almost literally in his hands. Yet, short of bodily kidnapping her, he couldn't reel her in. Not yet, anyway. He couldn't bear to let her walk away from him, but at this point, what choice did he have?

The funny thing was, he was pretty sure she didn't want to walk away from him, either. If she *was* Brenna Fallon, as he was dead certain she was, her insides had to be a mess right about now. He'd just dropped a hand grenade into her life. She had to have a million questions she was dying to ask but couldn't, not without admitting who she was. Or, to use another one of those damn poker analogies that seemed to be everywhere lately, folding.

Again, he couldn't be sure, since he hadn't watched her play very much, but he had an idea Billie Farrell didn't fold very often.

She'd paused, standing in the V of the open car door, and in that moment he heard himself say, "I'm going to be around awhile..."

She ducked down to give him her knowing half smile. "Right—for your sister's wedding."

He gave her back a huff of unamused laughter. "If you really want to hear the story, come by my hotel after work. I'll buy you a drink—or you can buy me one."

"A drink?"

"A beer...martini...something with an umbrella in it—hell, I don't care."

Her smile broadened. "How 'bout a Diet Coke?"

"Whatever turns you on," he heard himself say, and it wasn't something he was in the habit of saying.

"Where are you staying?" Her voice was both husky and breathless, and the frisson of awareness took another meander across his skin.

He gave her the name of his hotel, a good-size one located well off the Strip. She nodded. "I know where it is." She straightened and firmly closed the door.

Holt watched her walk away, watched a stiff November wind lift the blond feathers of her hair to catch the desert sunlight. And, after a while, let go of the breath he didn't know he'd been holding.

* * *

He was driving back to his hotel when his cell phone rang. Since he wasn't a big fan of people who tried to talk on their cell phones and drive at the same time, he picked it up and glanced at it to see if it was somebody he could ignore. When he saw who it was, he thumbed it on, said, "Hang on a minute…" and pulled into a strip mall parking lot. He turned into the first vacant spot he came to and turned off the motor, then picked up the phone again.

"Brooke—"

"Have you seen her? Is it her?" Her voice was high and anxious, on the edge of tears.

"I've just come from having lunch with her—"

"Oh God…"

"—and, to be perfectly honest, I can't be sure. She says she's not your sister, but…"

Now her voice dropped to a husky mutter. "I don't understand."

Holt sighed deeply. "Look, I'm pretty sure Billie Farrell and Brenna Fallon are one and the same. She's probably got her reasons for not wanting to admit it. I imagine it wasn't easy being on her own at fourteen. She's learned to be careful about who she trusts."

"Did you tell her—" Brooke expelled a breath in an impatient hiss and reined herself in. "Yes, okay. But the pictures I gave you—has she changed so much?" Her voice was wistful, close to tears again.

He ran a weary hand over his eyes; he was beginning

to feel the effects of a night without sleep. "Hard to tell. If I could just see her eyes..." He gave a huff of frustrated laughter. "But she wouldn't take off the damn dark glasses."

Brooke laughed, too, a small gulp. "I know, I keep watching the poker game over and over, screaming at the TV screen, *Dammit, Bren, take off the damn sunglasses!*"

There was a long pause, and then she said softly, "She has very distinctive eyes, Holt. Not like mine, or Cory's. Hers are...I guess they're what you call hazel. But they're sort of golden, actually. Almost the same color as her hair."

"According to Cory," Holt said, "those are your mother's eyes. Your brother Matt has them, too."

Billie was in her bathroom, huddled under the warm shower spray, trying to think.

She'd asked for the afternoon off, pleading illness, and since she'd never done such a thing before, ever, her boss had not only given it to her, but had expressed his concern for her health.

"Probably just a bug—one of those twenty-four-hour flu things," Billie had told him. And the truth was, she did feel kind of sick to her stomach.

She didn't know what to do. She really had not seen this coming. The thing with Miley, yeah; she always had suspected her past would come back to haunt her one day. She just hadn't thought the ghosts would come from so *far* in her past.

Every instinct she had was telling her to get the heck out of Dodge—she'd even gotten her old suitcase down out of the overhead storage in her parking garage, but had left it sitting empty beside the back door. Because what was the point? Holt Kincaid had managed to find her once, and he'd surely find her again, no matter where she ran. She couldn't go back on the streets where she could vanish into the legions of anonymous dispossessed; she wasn't fourteen anymore—she was a grown-up member of society, fully documented and therefore traceable.

What was she going to do? What *could* she do?

It was at that point in her panic that she'd headed for the shower. She did some of her best thinking in the shower.

So. What were her options?

Running would always be her first choice, but in this case, probably a bad one. Not only would it be futile, at best only postponing the inevitable, but there was the thing about *brothers*. Holt Kincaid had said brother*s*.

Admit it, Billie, you're dying to know what that's about.

And, the man with the answers is dying to tell you.

So why don't you do it? Go see the man, buy him that drink—or let him buy you one—and see what he has to say. What are you afraid of?

Afraid?

That did it. She turned off the water and yanked back the shower curtain. Grabbed a towel and scrubbed her skin rosy and her hair into layers of spikes, every movement jerky with anger. If there was anything in the world Billie hated, it was being afraid. She was done with being afraid. Done long ago with feeling scared and helpless. Knowledge was power, right? These days, Billie Farrell was all about having the power. Which meant she had to have the knowledge.

And the man with the knowledge was Holt Kincaid.

The ringing telephone dragged Holt into consciousness from the depths of a sound and dreamless sleep. He groped first for his cell phone, then realized it was the room phone that was making the racket.

What the hell? he thought. A glance at the alarm clock on the nightstand told him it was three o'clock in the afternoon, since it was obviously daylight. Too early for Billie to be off work. He picked up the receiver and growled, "Kincaid."

"Hey, you up for that drink?"

"Billie?" He sat up and swung his legs over the side of the bed, scrubbing the sleep out of his eyes. "Where are you?"

"In the lobby. What's the matter, did I wake you up?"

"Yeah, well…I didn't get much sleep last night." He was wide awake now, and his heart was going a mile a minute.

"So you coming down, or what?"

"Yeah, sure. Give me five minutes."

"Okay, I guess I'll be in the bar. Want me to order for you?"

"Make it the coffee shop," Holt said, swallowing a yawn. "You can order me a cup of coffee—black."

As he lurched into the bathroom to splash water on his face and run a comb through his hair, he was wondering one thing: Would Billie be wearing her sunglasses?

In the parlance of Vegas, he was willing to lay odds on it.

Billie would have given a lot to be able to keep her heart from pounding when she saw Holt Kincaid standing in the entrance to the coffee shop. But although she'd learned to control a good many of her body's natural reflexes, pulse rate wasn't one of them.

Schooling her visible movements to be slow, careful, deliberate, she picked up her Coke and took a sip, then watched over the rim of the moisture-beaded glass as he spoke to the hostess, who pointed him toward the table where she was sitting. She smiled as she saw the hostess's body language change in the subtle and indefinable ways of a woman in the presence of a very attractive man.

He was attractive, no denying that. Wearing the same slacks, jacket and open-at-the-neck dress shirt he'd had on this morning, he didn't look quite so out of place in the hotel restaurant as he had wandering among the potted plants at the garden center. But no matter what kind of setting he found himself in, she thought, Holt Kincaid wasn't a man to fade into the woodwork.

The hostess's eyes followed him as he zigzagged his way across the almost-empty dining room, and so did

Billie's. When he pulled out the chair opposite her, she saw that he had a bedspread wrinkle across one cheek, and something in her chest did a peculiar little flip.

Another thing she hadn't learned to control—yet. She definitely needed to work on that.

Holt settled into the chair and reached for the cup of coffee steaming on the table in front of him, gave her a little nod of greeting and drawled, "Miss Billie."

"Wow," she said, lifting her eyebrows, "that didn't sound like California."

He drank coffee, grimaced and set it down. "I said I *live* in L.A. I was born and raised in Georgia."

"Really. You don't have an accent. Usually."

"I left the South behind fairly early on. It still crops up now and again, I guess."

Most people would have missed the slight flinching of the soft skin around his eyes when he said that, but Billie didn't. And she thought, *Aha. He's got ghosts in his past, too.*

She filed the knowledge away for future reference.

"Sorry about your nap," she said, and her eyes kept coming back to the wrinkle mark on his cheek. She had the strongest desire to reach out and touch it. Why did it seem so poignant to her? Something about that mark on the supercool, iron-hard Clint Eastwood clone brought to mind images of unexpected innocence…or vulnerability.

He regarded her while he drank coffee, then said, "I wasn't expecting you this early."

"Well, here I am." She lifted a shoulder, not about to

concede how badly she wanted what he had to give her. Billie didn't give her opponents that kind of advantage over her, not if she could help it.

Holt didn't say anything, just watched her over the rim of his coffee cup. She fought down impatient anger and said lightly, "You were going to tell me a story."

His eyebrows rose. He set down the cup. "Just like that? No social niceties?"

She gave a little tiff of sarcastic laughter. "Social *niceties?* What do you want to do, put money in the jukebox and dance?"

Unbidden, the thought popped into Holt's head that dancing with Billie Farrell might be a very nice thing. Unsettled by the notion, he gave her a thoughtful smile. For a moment the air between them did the sizzle and crackle thing, and then he thought, *What the hell am I doing?* He cleared his throat, shifted around in his chair and frowned. "I'm just trying to think where to start."

"How about, who hired you to find…this woman?"

He nodded. "Fair enough. His name is Cory Pearson."

"Never heard of him."

"No," said Holt, "of course you haven't. But the story begins with him. When Cory was a little kid his dad went off to fight in Vietnam. He came back changed— nothing like the loving daddy who used to tell his little boy bedtime stories he made up himself. He was moody and withdrawn…started drinking heavily, couldn't hold a job. It was a familiar story at that time.

"Anyway, as time went on, the family grew to include

four more children—two boys, and then twin girls. When their father was having one of his spells of PTSD, it was Cory's job to keep the little ones out of his way while his mother tried to talk her husband back from whatever hell he'd gotten lost in. Finally, one night when the little girls—the twins—were about two, their father had a violent episode during which he shot his wife and then himself."

"Good God," Billie exclaimed.

Holt nodded, picked up his cup and found it empty. A waitress appeared to refill it. He thanked her, waited until she had left, then went on. All the while Billie sat without moving, without seeming to breathe, even, her face gone still and pale as death.

"Since there was no other family, the kids were taken by social services. Evidently, no foster family could be found to take all five, so they were farmed out all over the system. Eventually, the four younger children were adopted—the two boys by one family, the twins by another."

Billie spoke almost without moving her lips, and devoid of all inflection. "What about Cory?"

"He was older, about twelve by that time. Too old for most adoptive parents to consider. He stayed in foster care for a while, but ran away so many times trying to find his brothers and baby sisters, that he eventually wound up in juvenile detention. By the time he graduated out of the system when he was eighteen, his brothers and sisters had vanished—adopted and gone."

Billie muttered under her breath.

Holt nodded. "He was just a kid, and a known troublemaker at that. What could he do?" He paused, cleared his throat and wondered whether, behind those dark lenses, there might, just possibly, be tears in her eyes. Was it his wishful thinking, or did her mouth have a softness about it he hadn't seen before?

As if determined to deny that, she cleared her throat and said harshly, "Okay, so he's hired you to find the four siblings—I get it. So why did he wait so long? Vietnam—that had to be…what, thirty years ago?"

Holt nodded. "That's a question Cory has asked himself. Mostly, I think he'd just given up. He managed to turn his own life around—went to college, became a journalist, a war correspondent. Fairly famous one, too—won a Pulitzer for his reporting on the Middle East wars. Was captured and held prisoner for a while himself." He paused. "It was while he was in an Iraqi prison that he met a man, an aviator who had been shot down during the first Gulf War and had been in that same prison for eight years. They were rescued together. Eventually, Cory married the man's daughter, Samantha. It was Sam who convinced Cory he needed to find his brothers and sisters. That's when he contacted me."

"Because you specialize in finding people." Billie's lips twitched slightly, too quickly to be called a smile.

"That's right." He spoke very softly now, too, watching her face. It occurred to him that she seemed to have gone a shade whiter, if that was possible. "As I said, I've found the two boys. Wade is a homicide detective in Portland, Oregon, and Matt is in Southern California—splits his year between teaching inner-city kids and being a whitewater rafting guide, which is quite a feat, considering a rock-climbing accident put him in a wheelchair a few years back. I also found one of the twins—Brooke. That was a couple of months ago. She told me—"

Billie stood up so abruptly Holt flinched back as if from an expected blow. "Like I said—can't help you," she mumbled, and there was no question about it now… her face was the color of cold ashes. She paused, then made a valiant attempt at a smile, obviously trying to backtrack, mend what for her had to be a catastrophic breakdown of her defenses. "Look…thanks for the Coke… Gotta go. Wasn't watching the time…I'm supposed to be—sorry."

She walked away, moving as rapidly through the dining room as the closely set tables would allow.

He didn't try to stop her, or follow her, either. He knew desperation when he saw it.

Billie managed to wait until she'd turned the corner and was out of Holt Kincaid's line of sight before she bolted. Fortunately, she'd played a tournament in the hotel and knew where the restrooms were. Even so, she barely made it into a stall before becoming wretchedly, violently ill.

Thankfully, the restroom was empty. She threw up until she had nothing left in her stomach, then collapsed onto the cold tile floor, pulled her knees to her chest and wrapped her arms around them in a vain effort to stop the shaking. The pressure of sobs was like an iron fist squeezing her chest, and she hauled in air in great gulps and clenched her teeth so hard in her determination to hold them back, her jaws screamed in agony. She tore off her sunglasses and dug the heels of her hands into dry, burning eye sockets. But no matter how hard she pressed, no matter how viciously she tried to scrub them away, the images came. Images she thought she'd blocked out of her mind forever. Memories of pain and fear and humiliation and shame.

Brooke...oh, Brookie, I'm so sorry. I'm so sorry. I'm so sorry...

Chapter 4

Holt was trying to decide whether he'd just had a major break in his case, or blown it completely. One thing he did know: He was never going to be able to figure out Billie Farrell or anticipate her reactions, so he might as well quit trying.

Cory Pearson's story had shaken her, no doubt about that. And if it had finally sunk in that she had three brothers she didn't know about, he could have expected some degree of shock. Given the color of her complexion, he wasn't all that surprised she'd felt the need to make a hasty exit.

But he hadn't expected her not to come back.

He'd waited for her for nearly an hour, nursing his

cup of coffee and smiling at the waitress whenever she appeared anxiously at his elbow. He'd figured once Billie regained her composure she'd have a jillion questions—or at the very least, be ready to stand fast on her denial of any relationship to his client. Finally, accepting the fact that his quarry had slipped away, he'd signed his tab and gone back to his room to plan his next move.

He was sitting on the edge of the bed gazing at the wooden skewer in its napkin nest and trying to calculate the odds a lab might be able to get a reading on Billie's DNA from it, when a knock came on the hotel room door. His heart jolted and skittered around a bit, but he was pretty sure his voice was calm as he called out, "Yeah, who is it?"

When he heard a gruff, "It's me—Billie," his heartbeat settled down to a hard, heavy rhythm he could feel in the bottom of his belly.

He opened the door and she pushed past him without a word, her momentum carrying her into the middle of the room, where she paused and looked around her as if she wasn't quite sure where she was or how she'd come to be there. Naturally, she was still wearing the shades.

He closed the door and walked around her, touching her elbow as he turned to face her. She flinched away from him like a contrary child.

"Brenna Fallon?" he asked softly.

The dark lenses regarded him steadily, revealing nothing but twin images of himself. Below them her face showed no signs of emotional turmoil, only a kind of poignant defiance. "Used to be," she said in a voice full of gravel. "A long time ago. I'm *Billie* now. Billie Farrell."

"Okay," he murmured, nodding cautiously.

She spoke rapidly, vehemently, arms folded across her chest. "You got that? I'm not that person you're looking for. I wasn't lying." She sucked in air, and he wondered if her heart was beating as fast as his was. "I'm not that person anymore."

Again he nodded. Seconds ticked by, counted in those thunderous heartbeats, while he gazed at her and she stared back at him. Then he lifted his hands and gently took the sunglasses off of her face.

Her eyes blazed at him, molten gold like the just-risen sun.

His breath caught, and he felt as if he'd been punched in the stomach. He'd known it—known she was Brenna—from almost the first moment he'd laid eyes on her. Of course he had. But maybe he hadn't known it in his *gut*. Until now.

"You have your mother's eyes," he heard himself say in a thickened mumble he didn't recognize.

More seconds passed—he didn't know how many. Then without warning she reached up, caught his shirt collar in her fisted hands and pulled his head down and kissed him. Kissed him hard, with hunger and desperation and who-knows-what other emotions. And, at least for a while, gained his shocked and instinctive cooperation.

Might as well face it. He was never going to be able

to predict Billie Farrell's next move—or Brenna Fallon's, either.

She hadn't known she was going to kiss him—hadn't even known she wanted to. Kissing *anyone* was the farthest thing from her mind. For the first couple of seconds it seemed like the wildest, stupidest, most dangerous thing she'd ever done—and given her history, that was saying a lot. Adrenaline surged through her, prickling her skin and sending her heart rate rocketing off the charts.

Then...she *felt* him. Felt his mouth, silky soft on the surface, firm underneath...the warm, shocked puff of his breath, the solid bulk of his shoulders beneath her balled-up fists. And his response—she hadn't expected *that*.

She felt a moment of panic...thought, *I should stop this!* And discovered she didn't want to—for a number of different reasons. To keep from having to think about the bombshell that had just been dropped on her. But mostly...because it just felt so damn good.

Such a hard-looking man, and yet... *Who would've thought he would feel so good?*

She would have liked to go on kissing him a considerable while longer, but obviously he didn't share her desire. She became aware of his hands on her waist, felt them linger there a moment...then move with purpose to her shoulders. The pressure on her shoulders was gentle persuasion, at first, and his mouth still clung to hers in a way more wistful than hungry. Knowing what was coming, she made a soft, whimpering sound of protest, but his hands had already moved on to her arms, slipped along them until he could grasp her wrists. Before he could humiliate her completely by pulling her hands free of his collar, she gave up her grip and jerked away from him, furious and shaken. She would have fled, then, but he'd probably anticipated that, because he didn't let go of her wrists. And for a few seconds they looked at each other across their locked hands, both breathing hard.

Holt's eyes narrowed, and he said thickly, "You want to tell me what that was about?"

She lifted her chin and lowered her lashes, and injected her voice with a seductive bravado she was far from feeling. "Don't tell me you hadn't thought about it."

He gave her a sideways, wary look. "Uh…actually, no, I hadn't."

"Liar." But he went on looking at her, saying nothing. She felt cold and queasy. She knew her smile was congealing fast, and it was only pride that enabled her to produce a nice little pout and accompanying puff of laughter to go with it. "Okay, I think my feelings are hurt."

"They shouldn't be," he said dryly, "believe me. It's just against my principles to hit on my clients' relatives—or a woman who's emotionally vulnerable, for that matter." He gave a sharp little laugh and gallantly added, "But you sure don't make it easy."

She bit her lower lip as she smiled up at him and turned her wrists experimentally in his grasp. "You didn't hit on me, I hit on you. And who says I'm 'emotionally vulnerable'?"

He made a sound that was more snort than laugh and let go of her wrists abruptly, as if he'd just realized he was still holding them.

And it was only when he was no longer touching her, when she couldn't feel the warmth of his body and the strength of his hands, that Billie realized how much she'd been depending on those things—on *him*—for support. Now, without it, she felt herself trembling inside and didn't know how to stop. To her horror, she realized that what she wanted more than anything at that moment was for Holt to put his arms around her and hold her tight. She wanted to press her face against his chest and gather his shirt in her fists and breathe in the comforting scent of him.

Instead, she folded her arms across her chilled body, supplying herself with the hug she needed, and turned her back to him, preempting the rejection she knew was coming.

Oh no...where are my glasses? I feel so naked...

She would die before she'd ask Holt Kincaid to give them back to her, but...

You better do something about those eyes, Miley always told me, back when he first started teaching me to play poker. You're never gonna be a successful card player unless you cover those eyes. Every thought in your head is right there in your eyes.

"So it was just some kind of weird emotional reaction," she said stiffly, without turning. "I'm over it, okay?"

"Billie—Bren—"

She made a sharp gesture, cutting him off. "Look, I just came to tell you so you can go tell your client— Cory…whatever—that you found me. Okay? So it's over—case closed. Now you just go away. Leave me alone."

"Just like that?" His voice was soft now, and came from close behind her. A shiver ran down her back for no good reason. "Don't you want to meet them? They're your family, Brenna."

"I told you—it's *Billie*. That's who I am now. You got that?" She flung that at him over one shoulder as she moved away from him. "Family? Look, if you met my sister Brooke, you have to know about me and *family*. There's no way in hell I'm ever going back there. You can—"

"He's dead, Billie."

"What?" A small gasp followed the word, as if the spoken response had been automatic, and the shock a delayed reaction that came after.

Holt said it again, gently. "Your brother. He's dead."

When she slowly turned toward him, he watched her face, vulnerable and naked as a child's. Saw bewilderment, first, then something feral and raw he couldn't put a name to.

"How?" She whispered it, suspicious and wary. "When?"

"He was killed in a car crash a couple of years ago. Your parents, too. I'm sorry…"

But she had her defenses back in place now, and she hitched one shoulder only slightly as she turned away. "Hey—I'm sorry about my parents," she said gruffly. Then she went utterly still, and her voice seemed to come from somewhere else entirely—disembodied and devoid of emotion. "As for my brother…if there's a God, and any justice at all, he's in hell, right where he belongs."

"Don't you want to know about your sister?" Standing behind her, he watched her raise one hand to her face and wondered if she was wiping away tears, or perhaps feeling for the sunglasses that weren't there. "Brooke's had—"

She made a quick, jerky motion with the hand that had touched her face. Cleared her throat and said huskily, "I know about Brooke. It was on the news—about her getting arrested for killing her husband, and the mountain lion and all that."

"Then you know—"

"I know she's okay, that she's got a kid. She looks good—looks like she's doing okay." She whirled on him, suddenly, her face flushed and angry. "Look, what do you want me to say?"

Her sunglasses were in his shirt pocket. She looked so defenseless he was tempted to give them back to her, but instead he folded his arms over the pocket and the glasses and said softly, "She's got a new man in her life—a good man. I imagine she'd love to tell you about him…seems like the kind of thing sisters do." He paused. "She's dying to see you, Billie. *Brenna.* She misses you."

She turned her head and stared hard at nothing. He could see her throat work as she swallowed.

"And you have three brothers—real brothers, good, decent men, all of them. You have a *family.*"

Her eyes came back to him, bright with anger, and her lips curved in a smile of derision. "Family? You say that like that's supposed to be something great, right? Look, as far as I'm concerned, families are the reason for most of what's gone wrong in this world."

"Come on, Billie."

"*Don't.* Okay? Don't give me pretty speeches, because you just don't know." Her eyes were shimmering, fire and rain, although no tears fell. She paced a step closer to him, one hand upraised. "When I was on the street, all those other kids who were out there with me— why do you think they were there? Guess what? They had families. Families that *sucked.* Moms on drugs, dads on booze…I knew kids that had to leave home to get something to eat, or to keep from getting raped, beat up—or worse."

"Nobody said all families are perfect," Holt said evenly. "All the more reason to be grateful when you've got a good one. And you've definitely got that. *Now.*"

"Yeah? So *you* say." She paused, studying him thoughtfully, lips still curved in that mocking little smile. "What about you, Kincaid? You got a family? A 'good' one?"

She was good at reading faces, and his was kindergarten-easy. Once again she didn't miss the slight flinching around his eyes when he replied.

"No. No family."

"None?" She jerked back in feigned surprise, and inside she was gleeful…triumphant. *Aha—gotcha. So you have a skeleton or two in your family cupboard, Holt Kincaid.* "Come on. No parents? No brothers and sisters? Nobody?" She felt no guilt for taunting him. As far as she was concerned he deserved it for making her expose *her* emotions so cruelly.

Tight-lipped, showing none of his, he shook his head. "I was raised by my great-aunt, but she's gone now."

"Really." She watched him narrowly, her head tilted to one side. "So…what happened to your parents?"

He didn't reply, and his eyes had gone flat and gray as stones.

She stepped closer, and touched one of the arms that criss-crossed his chest. That, too, seemed hard as stone, but seemed to vibrate from some force deep within, and when she touched it, she felt the same vibration inside her own chest.

She looked up at him. "Hmm… So what was it? They die? Abandon you? Come on, Kincaid, I'll bet there's one helluva story there."

"I don't know you well enough to tell you that story," he said coldly, looking down at her without lowering his head so that his eyes were hidden by his lashes. His lips looked stiff and uninviting.

How could I ever have kissed them?

How could they have felt so good?

A shudder ran through her, and she shrugged to

hide it. She went on smiling, too, although she was seething inside.

I think...I hate you, Kincaid. Nobody makes me cry— nobody. But you came close. I'll make you pay for that.

She didn't know how, but she would find out what his story was, where he was most vulnerable. And she *would* make him pay.

And in the meantime, she still had an ace or two to play.

"That's easily remedied," she murmured, swaying seductively as she moved even closer to him, letting her hand slide upward along his arm, feeling the shape of warm, firm muscle beneath soft cotton.

Holt grasped her wrist hard. He couldn't seem to stop his body's response to her touch; all he could hope for was to keep her from feeling it. His smile felt hard and mean, but what else could he do? It was the only defense he had.

He hadn't expected this. Hadn't expected to be so attracted to her. Not just physically—he was confident he could have handled that easily enough—but in ways he couldn't explain. Ways that made him feel weak and vulnerable, even while some masculine instinct deep inside him kept wanting to protect and defend her.

As if, he thought wryly, this woman needed protection from him, or anyone.

"Is that something you learned on the street?" he drawled, hanging on to his smile with grim determination, even when hers wavered and he knew he'd hit a tender spot.

She wrenched away from him, the words she muttered under her breath a well known retort that invited him to perform a physically impossible act upon his own person.

"Billie—wait." Cursing himself silently, he managed to snag her arm before she reached the door. The look she shot him made a strange thrill ripple through his insides—something primitive, an irresistible challenge…a hurled gauntlet. His heart began to beat faster. He found himself recalling with uncomfortable clarity the way her mouth had tasted.

"Give me back my glasses," she said very softly, while her eyes seared him like molten gold, "and I'm outta here."

He released the breath he'd been holding. "Okay, look—that was out of line. I apologize." He waited for some sign she was willing to accept that, while the seconds thundered by in heartbeats he felt in his throat. "Don't go, okay? I really am sorry. And I do want to get to know you better…."

She glanced down at his hand, the one holding on to her arm, then angled a quizzical look up at him. And he realized his thumb was moving back and forth on the soft skin of her upper arm, stroking it. Caressing it.

Something lurched in his insides and he knew he was in big trouble. What he really wanted was to lift up his other hand and touch her cheek…then curve his hand around to the nape of her neck, cradle her head in his palm and kiss her—really kiss her, the way such a beautiful and fascinating woman should be kissed. He didn't do that, but he didn't stop stroking her arm, either. He watched his thumb caress the smooth, tanned skin for a moment longer, then lifted his eyes to hers and let his lips curve in a smile of genuine regret as he released her.

"…But not that way."

Liar.

She didn't say it out loud; she didn't have to. She could see the lie in his eyes and on his lips, written there plain as day. Plain as the numbers on a deck of cards.

She shrugged, folded her arms and sauntered past him, relieved to once again be far enough away from him so he couldn't feel her heart thumping. She flung herself into the only easy chair and said, "Okay…so I'm here. What do you want to know?"

He pulled out the hard-backed chair in front of the small table that served as both desk and TV stand, turned it around to face her and sat. For a moment he just looked at her, then leaned forward with his hands clasped between his knees. She found herself bracing— for what she didn't know.

"Tell me what it was like," he said in that quiet, almost whispery way he had that made her think unwillingly of lovers trading secrets in a tumble of sweaty sheets. "Out there—on the streets." He paused. She laughed nervously and looked away. His voice reached out to her…compelled her to respond even though she didn't want to. "How did you survive? How did you get off the street? Was it this guy, Miley Todd—your partner?"

"Yeah, I guess." She cleared her throat and shifted in the chair.

I don't want to do this. Don't make me go back there. Damn you, Kincaid.

But she knew she'd have to, if she wanted to win this game. Tell him everything. Go back there and live it all again. The pain, the loss…

Tell him, Brenna. It's the way you'll get him to go "all in."

She took a breath. "He found me at a bad time, I guess you could say. Or maybe a good time, I don't know." She forced a smile. "I'd just had a baby. Gave the kid up for adoption. So I was—"

He uttered a sharp obscenity and sat back in his chair. He didn't know what he'd expected to hear, but it sure wasn't that. Of all the things she could have said…

She was watching him, a smile playing around her lips but not even coming close to her eyes.

He rubbed a hand over his mouth and muttered, "How did it happen? I mean, were you—"

"Oh, it was consensual—more or less." She shrugged. "It was a cold winter…what can I say? You take warmth where you can find it, if you know what I mean. Things happen, okay?"

"I'm not judging—God, no." He exhaled, then shook his head. "I just can't imagine what it must have been like, to be out there alone, on the streets and pregnant besides."

"It was one of the better times, actually. I went to a clinic, and they got me into a shelter—a women's shelter, so it was pretty safe. Better than the others, anyway…I learned to stay clear of those."

"But you didn't stay. After…"

She seemed to have shrunk, somehow, sitting hunched in that big chair with her hands fisted on her thighs. Her face had a pinched look. She shook her head and he had to lean closer to hear her as she mumbled, "I got to hold her—just for a minute. It was a girl. Then they took her and I signed the papers and got the hell outta there. I just wanted to get as far away from that place as I could. Maybe you can't understand that, but that's just the way it was."

Maybe he didn't understand—how could he?—but he ached for her anyway. His throat ached. He cleared it, but still didn't think talking was a good idea, so he got up and paced restlessly to the window. It wasn't a spectacular Vegas view; his room did not face the Strip. Just an anonymous cityscape, darkening already to dusk, this late in November. He wondered if that cold wind was still blowing. In Vegas it was easy to lose touch with the world outside the hotels and casinos, but he knew there was a different world out there. Beyond the glitter and glamour of the Strip, Las Vegas was a city like any other, with its share of ordinary people leading ordinary lives, and criminals preying on both the innocent and each other.

"Miley Todd brought me here, to Vegas," Billie said, as if she'd read his thoughts. "I met him in Biloxi. He was playing poker in a tournament in one of the Gulf casinos, and I was working the main drag, picking up food money from the tourists doing card tricks...scams, actually. I guess Miley thought I had a good head for cards."

He turned back to her, discovering he'd lost his taste for asking questions. The images she'd already painted in his head were going to be tough enough to forget; he didn't need any more.

Funny—he'd never really thought about the term *empathy,* not until he'd run into the first of Cory Pearson's siblings, the Portland homicide cop, Wade Callahan, and the woman who'd recently become his wife. Tierney Doyle Callahan was an empath, a psychic who could read other people's emotions, and she'd met Wade while working with the Portland P.D. to catch a serial killer.

Meeting Tierney had gotten Holt to wondering whether he might have a wee touch of the empath himself, since he'd always had kind of a knack for getting inside the heads of the people he was searching for. An ability to think: *If I were that person, what would I do? Where would I go?* Not that he'd lay any claim to being psychic, but the fact was, a lot of the time he'd be right.

Brenna Fallon's story had grabbed him by the throat from the first time he'd heard it. He remembered vividly the clenching in the pit of his stomach when Brooke told him her twin sister had run away at fourteen to escape their adoptive older brother's sexual abuse. The photos Brooke had given him then had become burned into his brain, filling his nights with dreams of that fragile child-woman out there somewhere on some cold, mean street, vulnerable to every kind of predator and peril. Until a couple of days ago he'd all but given up hope of ever finding her, and then he'd had the incredible good luck to catch that poker game on late-night television.

Now…he slept no better, although it was a thirty-year-old woman's face that haunted him. Haunted him in ways he hadn't counted on.

"You want anything to drink? Or eat?" he asked, frowning, remembering the way she'd lurched out of the coffee shop downstairs, looking decidedly green around the gills. Chances were, he thought, she'd lost most of that Chinese food he'd bought her.

He knew he'd been right yet again when she smiled wryly.

"Yeah, actually, I am."

He picked up the phone, pressed the button for room service, then looked over at her and raised his eyebrows.

"A BLT on wheat and a chocolate shake would be fine."

He nodded, and she watched him while he gave the order, adding a cup of black coffee for himself. Noted the way his hair hugged the back of his head and receded—only a little bit and very attractively—at the temples. There were touches of silver there, too, and she wondered for the first time how old he was. Not that it mattered, she told herself. What did matter was that he was attracted to her, and she could use that to her advantage. She told herself the shiver of excitement she could feel running like a current under her skin was only the thrill of the game, the same excitement she always felt when she knew she was holding the winning hand.

He hung up the phone and looked over at her, eyes narrowed in a Clint Eastwood squint. She looked back at him, and the shiver beneath her skin coalesced in the center of her chest, a tight ball of warmth.

Take it easy, Bren, don't be too obvious or you'll scare him off. He's got scruples—who would've guessed a P.I. would have those?

She eased herself carefully back in the chair, elbows on the chair's arms, her hands clasped across her middle. "So, what now? You want to hear more about my misspent life?"

"No," he said, still frowning at her in that thoughtful way, "I really don't."

"O—kay." What now? She returned his gaze un-flinchingly, but inside she felt off balance, as if she'd missed a step in a dance. She had to pause an awkward moment in order to pick up the beat, and her voice sounded artificial even to her own ears when she finally said, "So, tell me about yours, then."

"Nothing to tell." It was brusque, a door slammed in her face with such finality she caught her breath in a small, involuntary gasp. He sat on the edge of the bed and leaned toward her, hands clasped between his knees. "What I would like to know," he said in a hard voice, "is why you don't want to even meet your brothers. Cory especially. He's been looking for you for a long time, you know. He was the one who protected you when you and Brooke were small. You were just babies, and he kept you safe when your father went on his rampages. He sheltered you both in his arms the night your father shot your mother and then killed himself. Without a doubt your father intended to kill you all. You'd be dead, too, if it hadn't been for Cory."

She lifted her shoulders and felt herself shrink into them, as if under the weight of Holt's steady regard. "Don't remember it," she muttered, angry with herself for letting him get to her. "Don't remember him."

He didn't say anything, and after a moment she got up and began to pace in the cramped room. Didn't want to, but couldn't seem to help herself. "Look, I don't know those people. I don't want to know them." Couldn't keep her voice from shaking, either. She turned on him, furious. "Damn you. I don't need this kind of hassle."

"Just…meet them." His voice was gentle now, and somehow that was worse. "Is that too much to ask? Just let me take you to them."

She bent closer to him, dangerously close. He was sitting on the edge of the bed, his face almost on a level with hers. She could see the pores in his skin, the beard stubble on his cheeks, the lines radiating from the corners of his eyes, the silvery shadings of blue in his eyes. It made him suddenly too real, too human.

A lump formed inside her chest and rose into her throat, and for one horrible moment she was terrified she might break down.

Tense with the task of holding off that threat, she

spoke rapidly, forcing words through clenched teeth. "Okay—you want me to go with you to meet these people? I'll make you a deal. You find people, right? Okay, then, you find my daughter. I want to see my daughter first. You find her for me, *then* I'll go with you to meet my so-called brothers."

"And your sister," he softly reminded her, looking deep into her eyes. "She wants to see you, too."

She couldn't stay so close to him, not for another second. She let out breath in a gust and straightened. "Yeah sure—whatever." About to turn away from him, she jerked back for one more shot, her finger upraised in a gesture of command. "But first, *you find my baby girl.*"

Chapter 5

Holt was dead certain Billie had no expectation in the world he'd actually be able to find her daughter, that it had only been her desperate attempt to put him off that made her ask such a thing. He was pretty sure he knew, now, what was making her fear a reunion with the sister she'd left all alone to deal with their nightmarish family. He didn't have to be psychic or even an empath to recognize the flash of panic and guilt in her eyes whenever he'd mentioned her sister. It wasn't the unknown brothers she dreaded meeting; he doubted that part had even completely sunk in yet. No, he was certain the person Brenna Fallon couldn't face was Brooke.

Unfortunately for Billie, she didn't know Holt

Kincaid very well. Didn't know about the resources and the network of contacts he'd established over the course of more than twenty years spent doing the very thing she'd asked him to do: Finding people. Particularly those given up for adoption, or the birth parents of adopted children. It was what he *did*, and he was good at it. He'd told her that, but evidently she hadn't believed him.

In any case, since she hadn't exactly volunteered her home address he was pretty sure she wouldn't be expecting him to show up at her front door less than a week after their showdown in his hotel room. Much less with her daughter's name and address in his shirt pocket. But here he was.

She lived in a modest stucco bungalow in a quiet neighborhood not far from the Strip. Built sometime in the nineteen fifties or sixties, he estimated. It was a neighborhood of mature trees and few signs of children, possibly in transition from its elderly original residents to young married couples buying their first home. Most homeowners, including Billie, had opted to forgo the upkeep of traditional lawns in favor of water-saving and maintenance-free gravel, although lining Billie's front pathway was an assortment of pots and containers filled with a profusion of autumn-blooming flowers and plumes of decorative grasses. A white-painted rail fence separated the front yard from the sidewalk and driveway, and a large tree with narrow gray-green leaves Holt thought might be an olive shaded the front entrance. The

November wind rustled the leaves above his head as he made his way among the flowerpots to the front door.

Nice, he thought, and wondered why he was surprised. She did work in a plant nursery, after all.

He was searching in vain for a doorbell and had just lifted his hand to knock when he heard a thump from inside the house. Not loud, not the sound of breakage, but as if someone had dropped something heavy, or possibly slammed a door. Immediately after that came the sound of voices raised in anger.

He threw a quick glance over his shoulder, his hand already going to the weapon strapped in a holster at the small of his back. There was a car—a nondescript gray Dodge sedan—parked in the driveway. He'd noted it, but had assumed it was Billie's. It hadn't occurred to him she might have visitors—or more likely *a* visitor, since one of the voices he was hearing was Billie's. The other was definitely a man's.

Given what he knew of Billie's past, Holt had some bad ideas about what might be happening inside the house. Not wanting to make a possible bad situation worse, he decided against knocking or calling out to her. Instead he flattened himself against the wall beside the front door and leaned cautiously to look through the window. He couldn't see anyone in the living room, but he could still hear the voices, which seemed to be coming from the back of the house. Keeping his head down and with his gun in his hands, carried low and to one side, he ran swiftly and silently along the side of the house, following a concrete walkway. At the corner of the house he halted and peered around into the back-yard. He could see more flower-filled pots and, adjoin-ing a covered concrete patio, a small free-form swimming pool, empty of water.

He could hear the voices clearly now. The man's voice, high and strained: "You *know* what they'll do to me. Are you gonna just let—"

And Billie's. "*Don't.* Don't you dare put this on me. I *can't help you.* Don't you get it? I can't."

"Hey—that's bull. You *won't.* And that's the kind of thanks I get? You little—"

"Don't threaten me, Miley." Her voice was vibrant with anger, and Holt heard a note of fear, too.

Billie Farrell—afraid? That got to him more than anything else. He tightened his grip on his weapon. Drew in a breath and held it, every muscle adrenaline-primed and poised for action.

"You and I are *done.*" Billie spat the words like bullets, in a voice that did not tremble. "I told you. After that last tournament. I paid you back. I don't owe you anything."

"You paid me *diddly!*" Miley was whining now. "What'd you make, a quarter mil? You give me a lousy twenty-five G's! What'd you do with the rest of it?"

"It's none of your business what I did with it. I don't have it. You got it? I can't help you. Now, get out of my house. And don't you *ever* come here again, you hear me? Stay away from me!"

"Jeez, Billie, all I'm askin' for—"

"Out...*now!*"

"This ain't over! I'm not—" There was a sharp exclamation and some vehement swearing, followed by, "For Chrissake, put that away—are you *crazy?* I'm going, okay? I'm *going.* Jeez..."

Footsteps thudded through the house. The front door slammed, and a moment later Holt heard the car start up in the driveway. Slipping his gun back in its holster, he swiftly crossed the patio, gave a warning knock, then thrust open the backdoor.

"Hey, are you okay—" The question died with a sharp intake of breath.

A few feet away, Billie had whirled to confront him, eyes blazing fire. Now she uttered a small, horrified squeak and collapsed back against the kitchen counter, one hand covering her mouth. In the other, Holt noted, she was gripping a rather large knife.

It took him about a second to get to her, and he was swearing vehemently under his breath as he gently took the knife—a serrated bread knife, it appeared—from her unresisting fingers. Then, in a little flurry of motion that could only have been spontaneous, she came into his arms.

What could he do? He dropped the knife onto the countertop and wrapped his arms around her. Which lasted about a second, barely long enough for him to register the fact that she was shaking, and that her hair smelled nice, and that her body felt incredibly good right there, snugged up against his.

She gave a furious gasp and thumped his chest with

her fists as she pushed away from him. "*Jeez,* Kincaid. What are you doing here? Are you friggin' *nuts?*" Her voice was shrill and breathless. She glared at him for a moment, then spun away from him, and as she did she caught sight of the knife lying where he'd dropped it on the countertop. She recoiled and jerked back to him, one hand clamped to the top of her head. "I could have— what if I'd—*dammit,* Kincaid!"

"I'm assuming that was your former partner Miley Todd." He kept his tone mild, figuring at least one of them ought to try to keep calm.

Her laugh was a sharp bark of anger. "Yeah…the man's a weasel." She turned back to the counter, picked up the knife, opened a drawer and dropped the knife into it, then closed it carefully.

Stay calm, Billie. You've already given too much away. What's wrong with you, throwing yourself at him like that? Since when do you need a man protecting you?

Oh, but admit it…it did feel good.

Yeah…too damn good.

She could feel him there, just behind her. *Too close.* If she turned now she could hardly avoid touching him.

"What did he want?"

"Money—what else?" She closed her eyes and willed him away.

Which seemed to work, because his next question came from a slightly greater distance. A foot or two. Breathing room at least. So why did she now feel off balance and precarious, as if she'd been left teetering on the brink of some great abyss with nothing to hold on to?

"So, what's his story?"

She had room to turn and face him now, so she did—carefully. He was leaning against the refrigerator, arms folded on his chest, regarding her with that narrow blue gaze of his. She leaned back against the counter and deliberately copied his stance. "You are the nosiest guy I ever met, you know that?"

He smiled. "Goes with the job."

She hadn't expected the smile. For some reason and without warning, a tightness gripped her throat. Unable to speak for a moment, she looked at the floor and gave a little sigh of laughter, then caught a breath and lifted her eyes back to his. "What are you doing here, Kincaid? I'm not even gonna ask how you found me."

Without a word, he reached into his shirt pocket, pulled out a folded piece of paper and handed it to her.

"What's this?" she demanded as she took it. She unfolded the piece of hotel stationery. On it, neatly printed in block letters, was a couple's name: Corrine and Michael Bachman. Below that was an address in Reno, Nevada. Below *that* was a name, circled: *Hannah Grace*.

Billie couldn't feel her fingers. She stared down at the paper. The words danced…shimmered…blurred.

She didn't know what to do.

I won't cry. I can't cry. I sure as hell am not going to

*throw myself into his arms, not again! But I don't know
what to do.*

"This is her—my daughter?" Her voice felt scratchy,
and sounded unfamiliar.

"That's her." His voice was gentle—damn him. It
would have been better if he'd been brusque. She could
have handled that. Gentleness…not so well.

"Huh." She shook her head, struggled to find breath.
Pulled air in, then let it out. "That easy, huh?"

"If you know where to look." His hands had a
strange, tingly feeling, an urgent need to reach for her…
touch her. Hold her. He kept them firmly tucked between his folded arms and body.

"Wow," she said, and he watched her struggle to
find something else to say and finally give it up and
just laugh, the kind of laugh that meant anything but
amusement. Her throat moved convulsively and his
ached in sympathy.

"Can I—" she said, at the same moment he said,
"Would you like to see her?"

And even though he knew it was what she wanted
more than anything in the world, he saw panic flash in
her eyes. "From a distance," he added gently, and she
nodded in a dazed sort of way.

A moment later, though, she did a startled double
take and said, *"Now?"*

"Sure, why not? You have the day off so might as well."

"How did you—"

"I stopped by the garden center looking for you

first. They told me you were off today. And tomorrow, too, right?"

"Yeah…" She looked down at the piece of paper in her hand, fingered it restlessly, as if she didn't know what to do with it. Then she tossed it onto the countertop. "It's so far. It would take forever to drive to Reno."

Holt smiled. "Who said anything about driving?"

Billie stood on the sun-bleached airstrip and watched the red-and-white plane taxi toward them, sending up puffs of dust that went spiraling away in the midday breeze. The plane looked way too small to hold three people. It looked like a child's toy.

She sucked in a breath, which did nothing to relieve the knots in her stomach.

It's happening too fast. It's too much, first Miley shows up, and now this.

Her past was catching up with her. More than that. It seemed suddenly to be looming over her like a gigantic tsunami wave, one breath away from drowning her. She felt dizzy, a little sick. She wanted to lie down somewhere and go unconscious for a while until the world slowed down, or she caught up with it.

She'd had the same feeling before. Too many times before. In the past, her remedy for this feeling would be to run, to just *go,* get away as far and as fast as she could.

I should have gone. Should have left the day I saw him there in the garden center, picking out plants. I knew he didn't belong there. I knew he was bad news.

So, why don't you go now? What's stopping you? Nobody's forcing you to get on that ridiculous toy airplane.

The plane coasted to a stop. Beside her, Holt touched her elbow, then went jogging out onto the packed-earth runway. The plane's single prop slowed and finally stopped, and the door opened and the pilot crawled out onto the wing, then jumped to the ground. He ambled over to meet Holt, and the two men clasped hands, then went in for the brief back-thumping that passes for hugging among guy-friends. Then Holt turned and beckoned to Billie.

She hauled in another breath she didn't seem to have room for.

Why don't I go? There's the answer, right there. I hate it, but it's there and there's nothing I can do about it. It's him—Holt Kincaid. What good would it do me to run? He'd only find me again. I can't escape the man.

And somewhere way in the back of her mind a voice she didn't want to listen to was saying, *Why would you want to?*

"I want you to meet my friend Tony," Holt said, reaching out to touch her arm, drawing her closer. "He's the man who's going to take us to Reno."

The man's hand swallowed hers and his smile seemed to light up the already sun-shot day. He reminded her of a Humvee—big and square and formidable, and he made her feel safe.

She nodded and managed a breathless, "Hi," and his whiskey-colored eyes crinkled with laughter.

"Hey—it's all good. I promise I'll get you there and back in one piece." He clapped his hands together like an enthusiastic child and beamed at her. "Okay. Are you ready? Well, hop in, then.

"You get to ride shotgun," he told her as he guided her up onto the wing. To Holt he added, "Sorry, buddy—you get to sit on the floor. I took out the passenger seats to make room for my equipment and extra fuel."

"I guess it's a good thing it's not a long flight," Holt said dryly.

"I'm a photojournalist," Tony explained to Billie. "So I've got lots of stuff. Plus, the places I go don't always have convenient airfields with fuel pumps."

"Uh-huh," Billie said. She had her head inside the plane now, and was trying not to stare at the array of instruments across the front of the cockpit. She glanced back at the two faces smiling encouragement at her from below. "Um…I can sit on the floor. Really. I wouldn't mind." *Because back there where nobody can see me, maybe I can curl up in a fetal ball and stay there until we land….*

The two men chuckled, as if she'd said something funny.

"Never flown in a small plane before, huh?" Tony's eyes were warm with sympathy. "You'll be fine—I promise not to do anything crazy. Just buckle up…settle back and enjoy the ride, okay?"

"Okay." She gave him the smile he seemed to want, but the truth was, she did feel a little better. It was just something about him, the laid-back, effortless charm that made her forget about thirty seconds after meeting him that he had a face resembling a cross between a bouncer in a biker bar and a benevolent pit bull terrier. Whatever it was, she just had the feeling she could trust him.

As she settled into the passenger seat she looked over her shoulder and found Holt's eyes on her. Something in their watchfulness made a shiver go through her.

What about him? Do I trust him?

Why do I have to ask myself that? I must trust him, or I wouldn't be making this insane trip with him, would I?

If that's so, why does he make me feel...off balance? Unsure of myself? Scared?

Yes—scared. The truth was, Holt Kincaid frightened her. She hadn't thought of it quite like that, until she'd met Tony and realized the difference. Tony was a stranger to her, and yet, he made her feel safe. Rather like having a big brother...

Brother? Wait. No. Could this be...

The thought popped into her head, and just as quickly she rejected it. No, this man had the deep-mahogany skin tones and broad cheekbones that hinted at Native American origins, and besides, Holt had told her her brothers' names, and none of them had been Tony.

Still...the thought lingered. *Brother...I have brothers? Holt says I do. Real ones.*

And from the thought, as if from a planted seed, feelings began to grow inside her. Feelings she couldn't define, because she'd never felt them before. Feelings...

like warmth, and…comfort, and whatever the opposite of loneliness was called. Perhaps belonging?

All this went through her mind in the few seconds while she stared into Holt Kincaid's eyes. Then she drew a shaken breath and turned in the high-backed red velveteen seat and pulled her seat belt across her chest. And as the little airplane's engines caught and the seat beneath her began to vibrate, as Tony donned headphones and muttered into a radio microphone, inside her chest she quivered with excitement and apprehension and anticipation, and something that felt—impossibly—like joy.

At the same moment, on the floor behind her seat, strapped uncomfortably to the wall of the passenger compartment, Holt was wishing he'd never gotten Billie to take off her sunglasses. Those eyes of hers…he'd never seen anything quite like them. And as the Piper Cherokee shot down the runway and lifted into the cloudless Nevada sky, he knew the hollow feeling in his stomach had nothing to do with the abrupt change in altitude.

No use kidding himself—it wouldn't change the fact that the unthinkable had happened. He was in grave danger of falling in love with his client's baby sister. Falling in love with a woman with two names and more complications than anybody he'd ever met. A woman he wasn't sure he'd ever be able to completely understand. How was that even possible?

Not that he knew much about it—falling in love—from personal experience, anyway. It hadn't ever happened to him before, and he'd come to believe, with pretty much equal parts regret and relief, that it never would.

Right now, with his backside growing numb from its contact with the floor of a vintage Piper Cherokee, he couldn't even recall exactly when it had happened. Looking back, it almost seemed as if it had been that very first moment, when he'd first caught a glimpse of her face on his TV screen, half hidden behind a pair of mirrored sunglasses, and there'd been that electric shiver across his skin. He'd been carrying her picture around in his pocket for weeks, but the sense of recognition was more than that.

But he doubted that was true. It only *seemed* like he'd known her, or at least had been looking for her, all his life.

Fanciful stuff, and he was not a fanciful man. Nor did he believe in things like fate and destiny. No, he told himself, this was just biology, a simple matter of chemistry, which was maybe even harder to explain.

With her face pressed against the side-window glass, Billie watched the strangely colorful desert terrain give way to the curving avenues of Reno's suburbs. She's down there…somewhere, she thought. *Hannah Grace. My daughter.*

Why did I ever ask him to find her? What was I thinking?

Why don't I feel anything?

It was as if her subconscious mind had thrown up a firewall around her emotions. Self-preservation?

But I want to feel something. I should feel some-thing...shouldn't I? What's wrong with me? I'm going to see my child. My baby. She was a part of me, and I gave her away. And I can't feel anything!

She could remember feeling. She remembered that day...remembered the awfulness of it. But it was only a *memory* of pain, not the feeling of it.

"She had dark hair," she said, and was vaguely surprised to discover she'd spoken aloud. Tony looked over at her, and his warm-whiskey eyes were hidden behind aviator's sunglasses. "I remember being surprised by that," she told him, not really knowing why she did. "That she could have dark hair, you know? Because I don't."

"Lots of babies have dark hair when they're born," Tony said. "Then it falls out and grows in a whole different color. So you can't tell anything by that. She could have blond hair now. You never know."

She gave a laugh that hurt, then drew a shaky breath. After a moment she looked over at him and said, "You sound like you know a lot about babies. Do you have kids?"

He shook his head, but smiled. "Not yet. I've just got a whole bunch of sisters with kids—lotsa nieces and nephews. I'm planning to, though." And his smile seemed to glow with warmth and promises and secret intimacies.

"So you're married?" Billie asked, wondering why the smile of a man so obviously in love should make her feel wistful.

Tony chuckled, a sound that matched his smile. "Not yet. Planning to be, though."

She drew another uneven breath and forced a smile. "She must be somebody special," she murmured, wishing it didn't sound so trite when she meant it with all her heart.

She wondered why he laughed, then, as if he knew a delicious secret.

The airfield north of Reno was much larger than the dirt airstrip in the desert near Las Vegas. Since it had once been an air force base and now served as home to the air tankers used in fighting forest fires in the nearby Sierra Nevada Mountains, its runways were long, wide and smooth—a factor for which Holt's backside gave thanks. Tony guided the Cherokee to a flawless landing, then taxied onto the expanse of tarmac where they were to park. Before leaving Las Vegas, Holt had called and arranged for a taxi to meet them, and he could see it waiting for them in the parking lot next to the airport office building.

Tony cut the engine and turned to give Billie a thumbs-up and a smile. "See? Told you I'd get you here."

Holt managed to get himself straightened out and limbered up enough to open the door and exit the plane first, Tony being occupied with the unknown details involved in concluding a flight and buttoning down his aircraft. While Billie was slowly unbuckling herself from her seat harness, he gingerly stretched his legs and aching back, then turned to give her a hand climbing down, if she needed it.

But she was still crouched in the doorway of the plane, poised as if for a leap off a high diving board, and her face was bleached to the color of desert sand.

"Airsick?" he said gently, even though the gnawing sensation in the pit of his own stomach told him that wasn't her problem, not by a long shot. He held out his hand to her and added, "You'll feel better once your feet are on the ground."

She gave him a withering look as she crept onto the wing, then hopped, with a nimbleness he envied, to the ground. "I've changed my mind," she announced, glaring at a point somewhere off to his right. "This is stupid. I don't know what I was thinking. Take me home."

Her teeth were chattering. Holt took the jacket she was carrying folded over one arm and, while she transferred her glare to his face, slipped it around her shoulders. Her eyes seemed too big, too fiery for such a small, pixieish face, as if the heat and turmoil that fed them was trying to consume her from the inside out. He wanted so badly to take her face in his hands, hold it, protect it like some fragile, delicate blossom, soothe the burning with his kisses. He could barely contain himself, she touched him so.

"You'll be fine," he said in what he'd meant to be a murmur but sounded instead like a growl. To emphasize his words, he tugged the two sides of her jacket he was holding, giving her a little shake. Her sunglasses slipped out of one of the jacket pockets and fell onto the tarmac. He bent down and picked them up, unfolded and slid them onto her face. It was like closing a door on a roaring furnace.

He couldn't resist stroking the spikey feathers of her hair behind her ears as he settled the earpieces in place, and his voice held more gravel as he said, "Better now?"

The lenses held steady for a long moment, and then she gave him the ghost of a smile. He let out a silent breath and hooked his arm around her shoulders, and as he did he cast one quick look back at Tony Whitehall, crouched in the doorway of the Piper Cherokee, giving him the thumbs-up sign.

She didn't speak a word on the twenty-minute ride into Reno, just kept looking out of the window of the cab, keeping her face turned away from him.

When they turned into the residential neighborhood of curving streets and stucco houses of the northwest part of the city, Holt said in tentative encouragement, "Looks nice—nice trees…nice houses."

She nodded but didn't reply or look at him.

"Nice place to raise a kid," he offered, and she didn't reply to that, either.

He checked his watch, then leaned forward to tap on the cab driver's shoulder. "This is okay—pull over right here."

"You sure? The address you gave me is a couple houses farther on down."

"Yeah, I know. This is fine. Might be a few minutes… keep the meter running." He'd explained their mission to the cabbie before they'd left the airport, not wanting to alarm him when they might appear to be stalking a child.

"No problem," the cabbie drawled as he pulled in to the curb and shifted into park. "Long as you're payin' me, I got all day."

Around them the neighborhood was stirring to life. Cars pulled into and out of driveways and came and went along the street. Two boys on bicycles whizzed by the waiting cab; children's voices mingled with the slap of running footsteps on sidewalks and pavement. Doors slammed.

"School just let out," Holt murmured. "Shouldn't be long now." He was looking over his shoulder, through the back window of the cab, intently watching the children coming along the sidewalk in clusters of twos and threes, sometimes more. The boys were untidy knots of motion, hopping, whirling, punching, pushing, laughing, the girls more sedate, heads together, arms linked, giggling and sharing secrets. Here and there a child walked alone, head bowed over a handheld electronic gadget or cell phone, thumbs busily punching buttons, oblivious to all else.

"There she is," he said suddenly. He put his hand on Billie's shoulder and pointed past her, directing her attention out the side window to the three girls now coming into view a block away. "Purple pants, pink jacket—see her?"

Billie's head moved, a quick up and down. Other than that she seemed to have gone still as stone—except that beneath his hand he could feel her body quivering.

"She's blond," he said softly, his lips near her ear. "Like you."

She nodded again, and this time made a sound, a very small hiccup of laughter.

After that there was stillness, except for the cabbie's raspy breathing and the ticking of the meter, while they watched the three girls pass by their taxi with only a brief, incurious glance. Two houses farther on, the girl in the pink jacket detached herself from her friends with a wave and a little pirouette and ran up the driveway, her blunt-cut blond hair bouncing on her shoulders, to disappear inside the open garage.

Billie sat motionless. Holt caught the cabdriver's eye in the rearview mirror and nodded. The car moved away from the curb, moved along the street past the house where the girl in the pink jacket lived and turned the corner.

There was a soft sigh of exhaled breath as Billie turned from the window at last and sat back in the seat. Her head swiveled toward him. "It's a pretty name— Hannah Grace," she said. "Isn't it?"

Her glasses gazed at him, blank, bleak…empty.

"Ah, Billie…" he said, and then was silent. What could he say?

You touch my heart. You make me want to wrap you in my arms and keep you from ever again knowing heartache, loss, despair.

The words would feel awkward and sound silly coming out of his mouth. He wasn't a poet, a man comfortable with words and feelings.

He put out his arm and was only mildly surprised when she let him pull her close. Her glasses bumped awkwardly against his shoulder, and he reached across with his free hand and removed them. She nestled her face in the hollow of his chest and arm, but he knew by her stillness she wasn't crying. He wondered what it would take to make this woman cry.

Chapter 6

It was late by the time they got back to Las Vegas.

They had taken time out for a fast-food hamburger before leaving Reno, which was pretty much Holt's customary choice of cuisine, anyway. He had noticed Billie barely touched the salad she'd ordered, although she did help herself to a few of his French fries. Then, at the Vegas airstrip Tony couldn't let them go without getting one of his cameras out of the back of the plane and snapping a bunch of pictures, mostly of Billie.

She had been good-natured about it, probably figuring it was pretty much to be expected, given that Tony was a photographer. Naturally, she didn't know the real reason he wanted those pictures, which was that

Brooke, twin sister to Brenna and the woman Tony Whitehall planned to marry and start having kids with in the very near future, would surely have skinned him alive if he'd come home without them. That was a revelation both Holt and Tony had agreed would be better kept for another time…another place.

Billie hardly spoke a word on the drive back into the city. She hadn't said much during dinner or the flight from Reno, either, except to answer direct questions, usually accompanied by a distracted smile. And the closer they got to her neighborhood, the less Holt liked the idea of dropping her off at her front door and leaving her alone. He told himself it was because he didn't want to risk giving her a chance to cut out on him. They'd had a deal and he'd kept his end of the bargain, and now *her* moment of reckoning was at hand. He had no idea in the world what was going on inside her head right now, but he did know she had a history of running when things got rough.

But he knew in his heart that was only part of it, and that the whole truth was both simpler and more complicated than that. The truth was, he didn't want to leave her. Period.

He pulled into her driveway and turned off the Mustang's motor and got out of the car, expecting her to tell him he didn't need to come in, that she'd be fine, thanks for everything and good night.

She didn't say that. She didn't say anything at all, just walked beside him along the avenue of potted plants, up the steps and onto her front porch. Holt kept his hands in the pockets of his windbreaker to keep from touching her, putting his hand on her back...the nape of her neck. He told himself it would only have been a touch meant to give comfort and sympathy. Which was a lie. But even if it had been the truth, he didn't know that he had the right to offer her anything so personal, or that she wouldn't misunderstand if he did.

There was, he realized, a lot he didn't know about Billie Farrell. Or Brenna Fallon, either.

She'd forgotten to leave a porch light on, so there was only the dim glow of the streetlights to see by as she unlocked the front door, pushed it open, then turned to look at him.

"You want some coffee? Or a Coke, or something?" She'd thrust her hands into her jacket pockets, and her shoulders looked hunched and defensive.

"Sure," Holt said. "Sounds good."

He followed her into the dark house, across the living room and into the kitchen beyond. There was more light here, shining in from a porch light outside, above the back door. Without turning on the kitchen lights, Billie shrugged out of her jacket and dropped it onto a chair beside the dining table, then went into the kitchen's work space to make coffee. Holt took off his jacket and draped it on the back of a chair, then went around the table to look out the window into the backyard.

He was about to ask her why there wasn't any water in her swimming pool—just to make conversation—

when something crunched under his feet. He froze—outwardly. Inside, adrenaline was exploding through his veins. He knew what broken glass felt and sounded like when he stepped on it.

"Billie," he called quietly. But she had the water running and didn't hear him.

He was beside her in three strides, maybe less. She turned startled eyes to him as she reached to turn off the faucet, and he pressed a finger against her lips before she could utter the exclamation poised there.

"Shh," he whispered, his lips close to her ear, "I think you've had a break-in. Window's broken. Stay here while I check the house."

She nodded, eyes wide above his cautioning fingers, and he gave her neck a reassuring squeeze before he left her.

He took his weapon from its holster in the small of his back and began a room-to-room sweep of the house, gratified at how quickly it came back to him from his cop days, long years past. How natural it seemed. He cleared every room, closet and cubbyhole as he'd been trained to do, and when he was satisfied the intruder was no longer in the house, he retraced his steps to the kitchen, where Billie was calmly filling the coffeemaker as if nothing out of the ordinary had happened.

He switched on the lights, tucked away his weapon and reached for the phone that was sitting on the counter. She looked over at him and said, "What are you doing?"

"Calling nine-one-one." He paused, phone in hand,

to frown at her. "Somebody broke into your house. I'm calling the cops. And before they get here you need to check and see what's missing."

She shook her head and went on filling the coffee-maker, silently counting out spoonfuls of coffee. Her lips were pressed tightly together, and her movements were jerky with anger. When she'd finished counting, she set the coffee can down with a clank and snatched the phone out of his hands.

"Come on, Billie, you need to report it."

She stared down at her hands, gripping the edge of the countertop, the knuckles white knobs against the pale blue tile. She wondered how, just a short time ago, she could have wished to feel something. Now, she felt ready to burst with feelings. Feelings she didn't know what to do with, or how to even name. She felt angry, but didn't know who to be angry with. She felt sadness and grief and regret and longing and fear, so much of everything she wanted to find a hole somewhere and crawl into it, cover her eyes and ears and wait for it all to go away. She wished she could cry, at least, but she'd lost that ability a long time ago.

Then there was Holt. This man who'd made such a shambles of her nice, ordered life. This man taking up so much space in her kitchen she felt as if there wasn't enough air left for her to breathe. She wished he'd never happened, wanted to hate him, wanted to be angry with him, at least. And she was. *Oh, she was.* And yet, she couldn't bear to think of him going away now and leaving her alone.

"It was just that stupid Miley," she said between clenched teeth.

"You don't know that."

Having no other place to send it, she threw him a look of bitter fury. "I know, okay? I don't need the hassle. Let it go."

He leaned against the counter and folded his arms, and his calm only infuriated her more. "Why are you so sure it's him?"

She picked up the coffeemaker's glass carafe and rounded on him, words tumbling from her lips in a rapid mutter. "Because I know him. This is just the kind of thing he'd do. Hang around, wait for me to leave, then just…waltz in. He figures he'll find what he's looking for, and if not, well, he thinks he's going to scare me, at least. I told you—the guy's a weasel."

"What's the story with this guy Miley?" He asked it as he took the carafe from her hands and turned to the sink to fill it with water.

She stared at his shoulder, unable to bring herself to lift her gaze higher. She couldn't look at his face. Not now. She was too full of feelings already. In silence she watched him pour the water into the coffeemaker, set the carafe in place and switch it on. Then he turned to her, the question he'd asked repeated in his sharp blue eyes and upraised eyebrows. She caught a breath and said, "Do we have to go into this now?"

"Yeah, Billie, I think we do." He leaned against the counter and folded his arms, and she could see no quarter in his face, or hear any gentleness in his voice. "I heard him threaten you. He scared you enough that you pulled a knife on him. So, yeah. We need to go into it *now*."

For a long moment she just looked at him, her heart-shaped face set and angry, and Holt was conscious of a little thrill of combative excitement. But he was more determined than she was, or maybe she was simply beaten down by the emotional bombardment she'd taken today. Anyway, after a moment she closed her eyes, let out a hiss of breath and muttered something under her breath. Something that meant capitulation.

She postponed it as long as she could, though, opening cupboards and banging drawers and taking milk out of the refrigerator in angry silence. With everything assembled, she stood and glared at the gurgling coffeemaker as if doing so could make it finish its job faster and give her a few more moments reprieve while she poured and served. When it became clear that wasn't going to happen, she lifted her hands and let them drop, then turned on him.

"I was going to tell you the whole story—the other day, in your hotel room. You're the one that told me you didn't want to hear it."

"Yeah, well…" What could he say? He couldn't very well tell her what had been in his thoughts that evening…couldn't tell her how she'd haunted him, and how the pictures she'd painted of her life on the streets still did. "I didn't know the guy was still around. I thought he was past history."

"Yeah, well…so did I." She closed her eyes and he could see her fighting for control. After a moment she hitched in a breath as if girding for a difficult task. Clearly, he thought, this wasn't a woman accustomed to laying her troubles on someone else.

"Okay." She exhaled slowly. "He showed up about a week ago—a few days before you did, actually. He said he'd managed to come up with the buy-in for the big no-limit hold 'em tournament that starts in a couple days at the Mirage."

"I thought he's been barred from playing," Holt said, frowning.

"He is. Which is why he wanted me to sign up instead."

"Ah."

"I told him no," Billie said, her voice tight and vehement. "I'm done with that life. Don't have any desire to get back into it."

"I take it he didn't take no for an answer."

"He did not. Turns out he had a pretty good reason not to."

The coffeemaker chose that moment to announce the conclusion of its task with a belching, gurgling crescendo, and she turned to pick up the carafe. She poured two cups and handed him one, then set about doctoring her own cup with cream and sugar. She stirred, tasted, then leaned her backside once more against the counter, arms again folded, cup in one hand. She didn't move to sit down at the table, and neither did he.

Her eyes had a dark glint that wasn't amusement. "Miley always imagines he's smarter than everybody else. Or that everybody else is dumber, maybe. Anyway, he'd borrowed money from some pretty scary people to finance some scheme or other, and things evidently didn't turn out the way he hoped they would, so now he owes these guys some serious money."

"How serious?"

She drank coffee, frowned as she swallowed. "Seven figures."

"What? *Millions?*"

"Well, not *millions.* Little over a million, actually."

"Why would he think you could help him with that kind of money?"

Her smile was sardonic. "You don't follow tournament poker much, do you? A major tournament like the one at the Mirage, the winner will take home way over a million dollars. Even the runners-up get pretty big bucks. You know that tournament I was in, the last one before I quit? That was a fairly small one. I went out in third place, and my share after taxes was over a quarter mil."

Holt nodded. "I heard him say that. Sounded like he thinks you've still got it." He watched her closely while he sipped his coffee.

Her gaze hardened and slid past him. "Yeah, well, I don't."

"Why do you suppose he thinks you do?"

She gave a little huff of laughter and gestured with

her cup. "Maybe because of the way I live? Do I look like I just spent a quarter of a million bucks? Even if I paid cash for this house—which I did, by the way—and even considering I already gave him a chunk of the money—"

"Why did you? By the way…"

She drank the last of her coffee and put the cup on the counter. She felt calmer, now, at least. Talking about past history seemed to be helping take her mind off the present. She shrugged. "I guess…I felt like I owed him. It was the first time I'd played without him, and he'd put up part of the buy-in. So, I gave him his share and I figured that was it. We were done."

"So," Holt said, "let me get this straight. Your ex-partner gets in trouble with some loan sharks, he's desperate, he comes to you to ask you to get into a poker tournament in order to win the money to bail him out. You say no dice and he comes back, this time demanding money which he thinks you have stashed away from your last big tournament win. You tell him you don't have it, he threatens you, you pull a knife, he leaves…is that why you think he's the one who broke in here today? You think he came back looking for the money?"

She shrugged and held out her hands. "What else?"

He frowned. "Who keeps that kind of money stashed in their house?" She just looked at him. The lightbulb evidently went on, and he sucked in air. "Ah—I get it. You lived on the street…"

"…and, I was used to hiding my stash of whatever

I'd managed to acquire. Even after I met Miley, I didn't have much use for banks. He probably figures I'm still like that."

"Are you?"

She snorted, making it clear it was all the answer she was going to give him. After a moment he said, "So, it was true, what you told him? You really don't have the money to give him?"

She straightened with an indignant jerk. "Yes, it's true. Do you think I'm that heartless? The guy's a weasel, but he saved my life, probably. Of course, I'd give him the damn money. If I could."

Holt waited. The silence grew electric, and he knew she wouldn't tell him unless…

"Okay…sorry," he said, reaching past her to set his coffee cup in the sink, "but I have to ask. What *did* you do with it? The money?"

There was another long pause.

"Billie?" he prompted softly. She was so close to him…arms folded on her chest as she gazed intently at the toe of her shoe, scrubbing away at the vinyl tile floor. He couldn't see her face, just the top of her head, and her hair looked unbelievably soft. He lifted his hand and his fingers hovered…

Then, abruptly, she lifted her chin and shook back her hair and her eyes met his in defiance, as if she were about to confess a major sin. "I put it in a trust."

"A…trust." He felt a moment's confusion, jarred by how near he'd just come to touching her in a way he'd never have been able to explain, at the same time wondering why this was so hard for her to admit. It seemed a reasonable enough thing to do. Responsible, even.

"Yeah," she shot back curtly, "like, you know, a trust fund?" She looked away, then, and mumbled something he couldn't hear.

"I beg your pardon?"

Her eyes snapped back to him. "For her—my daughter. For Hannah Grace."

He didn't know what to say. Words seemed to pile up on each other in his throat, forming a hard knot. He shook his head, and she stared at him almost accusingly.

"It's why I asked you to find her, okay? So I could put it in her name. Her real name. It's for…you know—college and…stuff."

"Jcez, Billie…" His face felt stiff. He lifted his hand and rubbed it, but it didn't help much. His arms, his face, his whole body ached with the need to reach for her… hold her…help her.

He didn't know what to do. Only one other time in his life had he felt so powerless—and that was a time he resented being forced to remember now, if only by way of comparison. How had he gotten himself to this point? When had he become so tangled up in this woman's life? When had she become so important to him?

It occurred to him then that they'd been standing there looking at each other for quite a long time, in silence. And when Billie spoke, it was a moment before he could be certain he'd understood her.

"Would you mind staying with me tonight?" she said softly.

There was a part of him, then, that wanted to take a page out of her playbook—bolt, get the hell out of there, run for his life. He was not a man equipped to deal with emotional demands. He lacked, or so he had always believed, the ability to give of himself emotionally. The ability, in short, to *love*. And he'd always considered himself lucky because of it—love, after all, being notorious as the cause of pain, anxiety, insecurity, disappointment and so many other negative emotions he could never hope to name them all. The positive aspects of love, highly touted in song and verse, he'd always considered not worth the cost.

But now, standing here facing this woman, with her golden eyes holding a burden of anguish that seemed too great for any one person to bear, he was coming to the realization that he'd been wrong. Wrong about his own ability to love, anyway. And, at the moment, the hazards and burdens of loving someone still seemed terrifying, and to far outweigh the supposed joys.

What should he do? It was late; he knew he should refuse the offer, make his excuses and go. To leave her now seemed…unthinkable. But to stay with her, wouldn't that be taking advantage of a vulnerable woman?

Of course she was vulnerable—what other reason could she have for asking him to stay? He doubted she even liked him very much. She'd kissed him once, that's true. But only, if he remembered correctly, because she'd just gotten one helluva shock.

He'd been strong enough to walk away from what she'd offered him that night, hadn't he? What had changed? Why did it seem so much harder now?

The answer was obvious: *You've changed, Holt.*

Yes, but she hasn't. And she's had more than one shock today.

"If you need me to, sure," he said calmly, as he tried to pluck words of reason out of the chaos of his thoughts. *She's had a break-in, you idiot. She's uneasy about staying alone. That's all it is.* "Be glad to. I'll, uh…just bed down on the couch. If you've got a pillow and a blanket…"

She tilted her head and made a derisive sound. "Jeez, Kincaid, what are you, *twelve?*" Her eyes met his, bright and brave. "I'm not asking you to a damn sleepover. I don't need you to protect me. I don't want you to sleep on the couch. Don't you get it? I want you to stay with *me.*"

He didn't say a word, not one word. Just stood there and looked at her, and for once she couldn't read him at all.

Her first impulse was to hit him—anything to jar that stony expression off his face. Her second was to cover her face, hide her eyes. But she wouldn't give him the satisfaction of knowing how devastating his rejection was.

She felt cold, and any moment now she was going to start to shake.

It took all her courage not to look away and all her strength just to make her facial muscles form a smile. "Well, I sure as hell am not gonna beg," she said, and pushed past him, wanting only now to get away.

His fingers closed around her upper arm, and her response was automatic. She jerked back against his grip, and for a few seconds there was a kind of silent tug-of-war, her desperation against his greater strength.

Finally, he said in a low growl, "For God's sake, Billie—" and she gave a sharp little cry as he pulled her into a hard embrace.

It was what she'd wanted, what she'd asked for. She had no idea why she went on fighting him; her reasoning mind had deserted her. She'd managed to get her arms folded up between her chest and his and refused to let herself give in to the temptation his body offered… the warmth, the strength, the comfort she yearned for.

"Don't do me any favors," she managed to get out between clenched teeth as she struggled.

Above her head she heard a small gust of a laugh, and when she looked up in fury, his head swooped down with the quickness of a hunting hawk. She had time only for a muffled and wordless protest, and then her mouth was no longer hers to control. He simply took it… claimed it…made it his.

And she had no objection. Her reason had already fled, and the same primitive imperatives that had made her fight him so mindlessly now compelled her to surrender. She felt herself growing weak and soft, and all her muscles becoming pliant. Her head fell back because her neck would no longer support it, but that was all right, because his hand was there to provide a cradle for it instead. Of their own accord her arms abandoned their barricade and crept around him like soldiers quitting the battlefield. And it was then, when her guard had been vanquished and she was left defenseless, that she felt it begin…the insidious invasion of emotions she'd been holding at bay for so long. First the ache…in another moment there would be tears.

I can't…I can't.

From somewhere, some reserve she didn't know she had, she found the will to pull herself back from the edge. Back…from the brink, yes, but not from *him*. No…because he felt too good, and she needed him too much.

And so, finding her mouth once again hers to control, she now gave it up to him. And remembered as she did how good he'd felt before when she'd kissed him. And wondered why she'd waited so long to kiss him again.

Her senses returned and they brought her pleasure, something she'd almost forgotten these past few days, and was surprised she could still experience. He smelled good…that elusive aftershave she'd noticed before, and the warm, earthy scent that was essentially, unmistakably *male*. He tasted pleasantly of the coffee they'd both been drinking. Her ears were filled with muted sounds, like the throbbing of distant drums…heartbeats and soft sighs and murmurs, and the *shush* of skin on skin. But mostly, the sense that dominated, that ruled, that overwhelmed, was *feeling*.

Every nerve ending in her body seemed to be alive and humming, quivering with eagerness for his touch.

And everywhere he touched her the pleasure was almost too intense to bear. So intense it brought tears to her eyes, and because she could not, *would not* cry, she laughed instead. A soft little gulp of laughter, caught in the sweet warmth of his mouth.

She felt his lips curve against hers in an answering smile, and she lifted one hand to touch his face. Her fingertips tingled exquisitely from their contact with the roughness of beard and the vibrant warmth of skin beneath, and her smile blossomed against his. She was shaking now, with silent laughter that was her only available release for the emotions that theatened to overwhelm her, and she felt his hand touching her face in much the same way she touched his.

It seemed a long time that they remained like that, lips touching, alternately forming smiles and kisses, fingertips exploring the vibrant, constantly changing landscape of each other's faces, bodies melding so naturally together she almost didn't notice the intimate ways they'd begun to shift and cling.

Then he let a breath out, long and slow, and his hand moved to cup her cheek, fingertips combing into her hair as he lifted his head and pressed a kiss to her forehead. She tensed then, waiting for him to release her, wondering how she'd bear it when he did. But instead he whispered words against her sweat-damp skin.

"Does this feel like I'm doing you a favor?"

Chapter 7

She needs me, Holt thought. *That's all this is.*

She needs me, he told his conscience, *and I'm not walking out on her.*

Gotcha, his conscience replied. *Reading you loud and clear.*

For a while then, blessedly, he didn't have to think at all. Kissing Billie, he was discovering, was a full-time occupation, an all-encompassing pleasure, one that involved every part of him, including his brain. *And your heart, too? Yeah, what about that, Holt?*

But that, too, was something he didn't have to think about. At least, not then.

That fascinating mouth of hers, with its impish little

up-turn at the corners…who would've thought it could feel so lush and ripe and full of sweetness? And her hands—card-player's hands with their nimble fingers—no surprise that they should be so clever, but who would've thought they could also be gentle, almost tender in the way they touched his face. In stature she was petite, her body small and compact, well-muscled and tidy…but who would've thought she could feel so soft, and fill his arms so completely.

Then, once again they were breathing in ragged little gusts of air, clinging to each other, and Holt wondered if she was trying as hard as he was not to show how shaken she felt. If she was wondering, as he was, what to do next.

About then was when she said, "Okay," and cleared her throat, pressed her palm against his chest and stared at it. He could see her forehead wrinkle with a frown.

"Yeah," he said, and cleared his throat, too, not really helping much.

"This is the really awkward part," she said, and valiantly lifted her face to meet his eyes. "I don't suppose you, uh…came prepared for this. I mean, I understand if you don't have anything, but the thing is, I'm pretty sure I don't. I'm covered for the pregnancy thing—yeah, learned my lesson there—and I'm clean, too. Had myself tested before Hannah Grace was born, and I've been careful since, but I don't expect you to just trust me. I mean, you'd have to be pretty stupid to—"

"Billie," he said, "shut up." He kissed her again, but

a shorter time than before. When he lifted his head she started to say something else, so he kissed her again, for a lot longer, and this time when he released her mouth she just licked her lips and stared at him, slightly cross-eyed.

"You'd be stupid to trust me, too," he said softly, "but I think we're both in luck. I drove down from Reno and came straight here this morning. I've got my overnighter in the car. I'm pretty sure there's something in there."

She was gazing at him in wonder. Her dimples flashed, and his heart gave a little leap, the way it did when he caught a glimpse of a deer dashing across Laurel Canyon Boulevard in the early, early morning.

"Hold that thought," he murmured, then touched a kiss to the tip of her nose and left her.

All the time he was getting his suitcase out of the Mustang, locking up, heading back to the house, he refused to let himself think about anything except what he was doing at that moment in time. *Don't think, don't analyze…stay in the here and now.* That's what he told himself whenever a glimmer of thought tried to sneak past his mental firewalls: *Here and now. That's all that matters.*

Back in Billie's house, he found she'd turned off the lights in the kitchen. Following the glow from the hallway, he made his way to its source, which was the larger of the two bedrooms he'd cleared earlier while checking for intruders. He'd noticed then that although it lacked frills, it was a distinctly feminine room, done in neutral tones of cream and tan, with accents of black and green. There were plants near the windows, which were curtained now against the darkness, and Audubon prints and Ansel Adams photographs in simple frames on the walls. Now, with Billie added to the setting, he realized how perfectly the room suited her. And what an intimate thing it was, to share that room with her. He wondered if she knew.

She was standing beside the bed, which was neatly made, with an assortment of throw pillows casually arranged on top of the spread. The only light came from the lamp on the table beside the bed, which she'd evidently just switched on. She lifted her head and smiled at him, but without dimples.

"Okay, Kincaid, this is your chance," she said in a tone that wanted to be airy, the tension she was trying to hide betrayed by only the slightest of tremors.

He set down his overnighter and returned the smile in a tentative way. "Chance? For what?"

"To change your mind." She turned to him, moving her body side to side in a way that suggested a wavering of will. "You know—the moment's passed and we've both cooled down…pulses steady. Isn't this where reason and common sense usually step in?"

"And have they?" When she only clasped her arms across herself and looked away without answering, he persisted gently, "Are *you* having second thoughts?"

She gave a sharp little laugh and brought her eyes back to him. They seemed to shimmer in the lamplight.

"I asked you to stay with me, remember? Because I, um—" She closed her eyes and struggled with it, and he took pity on her and mentally filled in the words she couldn't bring herself to say.

You need me.

"Billie, no, I haven't changed my mind. If you need me, I'll stay."

She looked at him for a long moment, smiling that little half smile, then slowly shook her head and whispered, "Kincaid, you are such a Boy Scout."

"Boy Scout?" He gave a surprised huff of laughter. "Don't think I've ever been called that before. And why is it," he added wryly, "I get the feeling you don't mean that as a compliment?"

"I do, actually. I haven't met that many Boy Scouts in my life…." She studied him thoughtfully, and her eyes seemed to kindle. He felt their heat from where he stood, two full arm's lengths away. "Who would've guessed. That's sure not what I thought of when I first met you."

"Yeah? What did you think of, then?" He realized they were speaking in low murmurs, the tone lovers use to exchange erotic suggestions under cover of darkness, though there was still that distance between them. A distance that seemed vast and unbridgeable.

"Harry Callahan," she said.

"Who?"

"You know—Clint Eastwood movies…Dirty Harry…" He burst out laughing—he couldn't help it.

"You know," she said, watching him with her head

slightly cocked, "I think that's the first time I've ever seen you do that."

"Do what?"

She gave a little shrug. "Never mind—it's gone now. It was nice while it lasted, though."

She turned to take the pillows off the bed, saying over her shoulder as she did, "Bathroom's across the hall—it's all yours." She didn't see him go.

She told herself not to think, but, as thoughts will, they came anyway. *Why am I doing this? I guess I know why, I know what I think is why, but why do I need him when I've done all right without him up to now?*

She began to undress, her fingers stiff and cold on the zipper of her jeans, tossing her clothes in the general direction of the dresser on the other side of the bed. It seemed too…intimate, too personal, to leave them lying where he would see them when he returned.

When he returns…

She tried not to think about how it would be. How he would look.

His body…

I wish he'd make this easier for me. He's leaving it up to me to call the shots. I understand why, but I almost wish he'd take the lead. Funny…who would've thought he'd turn out to be so damned nice?

I don't need him to be nice. I need him to kiss me again. I need him to hold me. I need him to not let me think….

She lifted the corner of the bedclothes and crawled between the sheets, shifting herself all the way to the other side of the bed to leave room for him. The sheet rasped across her goose-bumpy skin like sandpaper. She was shivering, and no matter how hard she tried she couldn't make herself stop.

Holt left the bathroom and crossed the hall, his shaving kit in his hands and images of Billie in his mind. Not voluptuous, fantasy images—he didn't have enough intimate knowledge of her body nor enough prurient imagination to provide material for those—but flashback images of her face in all its different moods, constantly changing, like a kaleidoscope. He didn't try to stop them. It was better than thinking.

He hadn't any expectations of what he'd see when he walked back into her bedroom, but even so, the scene that met his eyes jolted him in ways he couldn't explain. He wished there had been a camera in his mind, some way of freezing that moment in his memory. Not a scene that could be considered sexy or erotic, not in the usual sense: Her face—just her face, her body a surprisingly small disturbance beneath the covers—nestled in a pile of pillows, its features indistinct, its outline blurred in the soft lamplight though the colors were pure and vivid, like a watercolor painting on silk. But for a moment he felt a weakening in his knees and that odd dropping sensation in his chest, and the need to remind himself all over again what he was doing here.

She needs you, Kincaid—that's all this is. Be good to her...handle with care...and when the time comes, let her go.

She raised herself on one elbow and watched him walk toward her, wearing all his clothes and carrying what appeared to be a small toiletries kit in his hands. She searched his face for a hint of a smile. Instead, his eyes seemed to burn her, and she wondered how blue eyes could do that.

"I left the light on for you," she said in a rasping voice. "You can turn it off, if you want to."

He placed the kit on the table beside the lamp and looked down at her. "Would you like it off?" he asked as he began to unbutton his sleeve cuffs.

She shrugged, and he reached for the lamp. "No—wait," she said breathlessly, "leave it on."

Why was this so hard? Why did it feel so awkward?

Because you never asked a man to share your bed before. Always before, sex was something that just sort of happened, or it was his idea and you went along with it. It was fun and games. Or two warm bodies obeying a biological urge. Whatever.

So...why does this feel like something more?

Because you're using him, maybe? Because you have a conscience after all?

But if she did, it was playing hide-and-seek with her, ducking out of sight again as she watched his fingers work their way down the front of his shirt, then pull the two halves apart and at the same time free of the waist-band of his pants. It shouldn't have been a big thing to her, this first glimpse of his body, so the little hitch in her breathing caught her by surprise. She searched his face for some sign that he'd noticed, but his intent expression, the slight, compassionate frown, didn't waver. She caught her lower lip between her teeth and watched him fold his shirt in half and lay it on the floor beside the night table, then take his gun out of its holster, check it briefly, then lay it carefully on top of the shirt.

His body pleased her; with not much fat to hide the pull and tug of tendons and ligaments, she could see the way muscle moved beneath pale skin in sculpted patterns. She liked that he wasn't tan—which she thought showed a lack of vanity—and that the hair on his chest was beginning to gray a little, to match the silver at his temples.

"Are you always so neat and tidy?" she asked in a voice that felt unreliable, and was surprised when he smiled.

"No," he said, as he unzipped his pants, "but I do try to be a well-behaved houseguest."

She let go a small gust of nervous laughter. "Houseguest. Is that what you are?"

He didn't answer, but reached instead to turn out the lamp.

The bed jolted as he sat on the edge of it, and wobbled with his movements as he divested himself of the rest of his clothes, shoes and socks. She felt the cold caress of wind when he lifted the covers and slipped easily between them. She waited for him to reach for her, to come to her, and she thought resentfully, *Do I have to ask him to hold me?* She couldn't seem to stop shivering.

"Billie," his voice came out of the new darkness, "are you cold?"

"No," she said, furious. *Just hold me, dammit.*

He gave a little growling sigh and put out his arm and she scooted over into its curve. He drew her close to him and she nestled against his body, but didn't relax. He could feel her shivering, and her body's shape felt warm and silky but unyielding, like a sun-warmed sculpture in polished marble.

He'd never thought of himself as a sensitive person, but uppermost in his consciousness was the thought: *I want to do this right. For her.*

He didn't want to think about what that meant.

Though it was dark already, he closed his eyes. And though he'd never seen her body, he began to see it now with his hands…his fingers.

She was small—he'd known that. But beneath skin as soft and fragile as something newly born her muscles were firm, her bones strong. Woman-strong. His mind's eye followed his hand along the graceful, sweeping curve of her spine, down into the valley, then up the gentle rise…and the roundness of her bottom seemed custom-made to fit his hand. Moving slowly on, even the jut of her pelvic bone seemed soft to him beneath the velvet drape of her skin, and her belly, covered in that same velvet, quivered when he stroked it like the hide of a restless tiger. He rested his hand in the hollow below her rib cage and let his fingers play for a moment along the undulations of muscle and bone while she sucked in her stomach and her breathing hung suspended. Then, slowly, he raised his hand along her ribs to cover one small, round breast.

Small, yes…but it filled his hand to perfection. He heard her breath sigh between her lips, and realized only then that she'd turned her face into the hollow of his neck. The warmth of her sigh poured over his skin like liquid sunlight. Her legs were shifting, too, one knee drawing up to rest on his thigh.

"You're not shivering anymore," he whispered, stirring the feathers of her hair. She didn't reply. He counted the thumps of her heartbeat against his arm, then added, "It's okay if you just want to go to sleep. You've had a long day. You don't need to feel—"

"Hush up, Harry," she said. "Just kiss me."

After that it was easy. What was it about kissing this man, she wondered, that blew every conscious thought out of her head? When he kissed her a warm darkness seemed to settle over her, the darkness of a sultry summer night, and the air felt like melted butter on her skin. She heard only the hum of her own life forces, and maybe his, too, and the song they made filled her head and her whole being, as compelling, as hypnotic as the throbbing rhythm of drums. His mouth…his kiss…became her world, and she never wanted it to end.

But it did—it had to. And she gasped a breath, tangled her fingers in his hair and growled from the depths of her need, *"Don't…stop."*

"I won't," he whispered. His hands cradled her head; his thumbs stroked her cheekbones…her temples. His body became a blessed weight, an all-encompassing embrace. He whispered it again, into her mouth. "I won't...stop...."

Holt came awake with two realizations clear in his mind. One, he'd slept well and without dreams, at least none he recalled. And two, Billie was very close by. For a few moments then, he kept his eyes closed and let his other senses flood him with evidence of her presence: Her breathing, an uneven cadence to it that told him she was awake; a fresh, sweet scent reminiscent of flower gardens with a hint of toothpaste that suggested she'd been up and perhaps showered; a humid warmth that was simply woman, and uniquely *her.*

He opened his eyes and discovered she was sitting cross-legged on the bed next to him, hands clasped, elbows resting on her knees, watching him. Her eyes were dark and unreadable in the thin early morning light. His first impulse was to hook his hand around her neck and pull her down for a good-morning kiss, but because he was aware of the fact that she'd brushed her teeth and he hadn't, and that there was something vaguely wary about the set of her shoulders, he settled for a murmured, "Mornin', sunshine," instead.

She leaned down to kiss him, but in a brief, distracted way.

He muttered, "Hmm... Sorry—you smell good and I don't. Be right back..." and rolled out of bed and headed for the bathroom.

When he came back, she was still sitting where he'd

left her, wearing a T-shirt a few sizes too big for her that made it impossible for him to tell if she was wearing anything else underneath. But since it was obviously early, barely daylight, and she didn't seem to be eager to be up and about, instead of reaching for his clothes, he got back into bed, too.

She cleared her throat, a sound full of portent. "Hey, Kincaid…"

He turned on his side and pulled the sheet up over his hip, propped his elbow on the pillows and leaned his head on his hand. "Billie?" he said somberly.

"I want you to know something, okay?" Her voice sounded blunt and self-conscious. A suspenseful little pulse began to tap-tap in his stomach. She closed her eyes briefly and held up one hand. "Look, don't get me wrong— last night was great. I mean—" she gave a breathy laugh and her voice dropped an octave "—more than great—really, it was—" She looked away, obviously stalled, and he saw her throat move with a painful swallow.

The tap-tapping in his belly became his heart going thump-thump… "Billie," he said gently, "it's okay, spit it out." He offered an encouraging smile. "I sense a *but* in there somewhere."

She hauled in a breath that lifted her shoulders, and the words came out in a rush. "I just want you to know, you don't have to be afraid I'm going to be making, um, you know…demands. I don't expect you to say nice words…stick around…ask me out—stuff like that."

She paused, frowned, and he murmured a tentative, "Okay…" But she wasn't finished.

"I mean, look, let's face it, you're not a forever kind of guy, right? I just want you to know I'm cool with that. Because for one thing, I'm not a forever kind of woman, either." She gave herself a little concluding shake and her gaze came back to him, fierce and intent. "So—we straight on that?"

He gazed back at her. There was a weird, fluttery feeling in his chest, and he didn't know whether it was laughter or tenderness. He settled for a smile. "Yeah, Billie, we're straight. No forevers, no expectations, no nice words." He paused a beat. "Does this mean I don't get to tell you you're beautiful?"

She jerked back as if he'd insulted her. "You're making fun of me."

He lifted his hand and brushed her cheek with the backs of his fingers, ran his thumb lightly across her lower lip. "I'd never do that."

She licked her lip where he'd touched it. "I told you, you don't have to say things like that to me, just because…"

"I know I don't have to…just because. I can say it if it's true, though…right?"

She clasped her hands tightly together and hugged her arms against her sides like a self-conscious child, and didn't answer. What he wanted to do at that moment was take her down into the tumbled sheets and show her without the pretty words just how beautiful she was to him. Instead, he let his hand fall away from her and said softly, "I have one question, though. You don't know me all that well…so how do you know what kind of guy I am—forever-wise?"

She unclasped her hands and held one up, thumb extended. "One, you're not married." A forefinger joined the thumb. "Two, you've never been married." Another finger. "You're in your forties, you live alone—" her hand returned to join its mate in her lap, and she shrugged. "Obviously not somebody who's into commitment." She tilted her head. "Just out of curiosity, what happened?"

"What…happened?"

"To make you that way. I mean, you know why I'm the way I am. So, what's your story, Kincaid? Come on—give. It's only fair."

He just stared at her, his face stony, and her heart did a weird little skip-hop she'd never felt before. She wanted to reach out and touch his face the way he'd touched hers—a way no man had ever touched her before, that she could recall. She wanted to touch him like that and say the words that were in her mind.

Who hurt you, Holt? Who made you afraid to trust anyone with your heart?

"You're right," he said, just when she'd been sure he wouldn't answer. "It is only fair. So, here it is, my reason—my *excuse,* I should say—for choosing to remain unencumbered by…emotional attachments." His hand reached out for her again, this time to lie briefly on her shoulder, then brush lightly down her arm. And his eyes held hers like a hypnotist's, with that ice-blue gaze she was beginning to realize was anything but cold.

"I was five years old. I remember it because I'd just had my birthday party, and there was a pony." A smile flickered briefly. "I think that was the first and last time I was ever on a horse. Anyway, a couple of days later, my parents left me with a babysitter and went out to dinner and a movie, and never came back."

He said it so matter-of-factly, it was a moment before it registered. She did a little double take, then whispered, "What happened? Was it a car crash?"

His hand continued its idle journey up and down her arm. "Their car was found in the movie theater parking lot. My parents never were. They just disappeared."

She stared at him, appalled, half-disbelieving. "That's…crazy. People don't just disappear."

"Actually, they do—more often than you'd suppose." His eyes dropped to his hand, which had left her arm to brush across the front of her T-shirt where her nipples had beaded against the clinging cloth.

She shivered. "What happened? To you, I mean?"

"Well, my babysitter told me lies, at first. Everybody did. About how my parents had had to go away suddenly, but they'd be back soon. Eventually, I was sent to live with my mother's aunt. She was a schoolteacher—unmarried. She did the best she could, I'll give her that." His smile was wry, his eyes forgiving. "Let's just say she wasn't a warm and fuzzy sort of person." He shrugged in a dismissive way that didn't alter the smile. "She died when I was seventeen, and I joined the army soon after. When I got out of the service, I decided I wanted to become a cop—a detective—so I could find out what happened to my folks."

"And did you?" It was hard to keep her voice steady, with his roving hand straying downward, stroking lightly across her thigh…

"No," he said. "But I found out I was more interested in finding missing people than catching bad ones, so I quit the force and that's what I've been doing." He didn't say any more, and a certain wariness in his eyes told her he probably wasn't accustomed to saying even that much.

That awareness made her feel chastened and humble, at first. Even, in an odd sort of way, vulnerable, too. But then a new feeling began to grow in her, one she remembered experiencing only once before in her life—the day her daughter was born. Something so primal she couldn't even put a name to it. Or didn't want to. But whatever it was, it filled her with a new kind of power and purpose.

All the while this momentous thing was happening inside her, she was looking into Holt's eyes and he was gazing back at her. His hand was sliding under her T-shirt and finding her nakedness all open to him, his for the taking. First, she gasped…shuddered…melted. Then, with her new inner strength, whispered, "No…" and leaned over to find his mouth, and at the same time was unfolding herself, finding her way inside the covers to sink against him and lay her body full length on his.

He made a sound low in his throat and his hands were big and warm on her back, stroking downward to hold her buttocks, then on to her thighs. But when he urged them apart, she murmured once more, "No…" mingling the word with the dark, sweet essence of his mouth. And then she slid down his body, slowly, kissing every part of him she met on the way, her heart growing quivery at the incredible sleekness of his skin. His hands were light on her sides, letting her slip between them, and his breath escaped him in the gentlest of sighs when she nestled her face in his warm, damp hair and kissed him there.

When he could take no more, he pulled her up to him and lifted his own body to meet her, and they found each other like old lovers after too long a time apart. He wrapped his arms around her, one low on her spine, the other cradling her head, and she brought her legs around his waist and arched to press her torso against his, nesting her breasts in the tickling softness of his chest hair.

Her mouth found his and she opened to him with no reservation at all, and would have gladly lost herself there, but for the sharp gasp that rushed from her throat when he seated himself deep inside her. He caught the gust of breath in his own mouth and held them both still, feeling the off-rhythm thumping of their combined heartbeats, until one or the other—maybe both—of them began to tremble.

Then he tore his mouth from her and in a rasping whisper said, "Billie…I—"

And for the third time she said it, a low, guttural

sound from deep in her throat. "*No*—no words. Just… make love to me."

"I will…I am…do you feel me loving you?"

And she answered, "Yes…yes…yes…" until she began to shake with dizzy laughter, the kind that sometimes comes with tears.

The next time they woke it was noon, or almost. This time hunger drove them out of bed and back to the kitchen, where a chilly November breeze was blowing through the broken window. While Billie made coffee, Holt taped a flattened cardboard cereal box over the hole, then turned on the noontime news.

"I usually eat peanut butter toast for breakfast," Billie called from the other side of the counter. "Is that okay with you?"

"Yeah…fine," he said absently, watching the crawl across the bottom of the television screen. He heard the thump-click of the bread being pushed down in the toaster and turned to say over his shoulder, "Hey, there's an Amber Alert."

She was coming toward him, rounding the end of the counter carrying a steaming cup of coffee, smiling. Her eyes went past him to the screen, and the smile seemed to dissolve into a look of utter bewilderment. "Holt?" she said, with almost no sound. The cup in her hands began to wobble, and he snaked out a hand and rescued it just in time to keep it from crashing to the floor.

He was licking his hand where the scalding coffee

had slopped over and burned it when he turned back to the news broadcast. Then he no longer felt the scald. He felt as if all the air in his body had been sucked out of him.

Billie moved beside him in stunned silence, and together they stared at the face on the screen…the face of a little girl about ten years old, a little girl with blond hair and magical golden eyes.

Chapter 8

"*Hannah Grace Bachman disappeared this morning while walking to school in this quiet suburban neighborhood just northwest of Reno. She was last seen wearing…*"

"This can't be a coincidence," Holt said unevenly. "Who do you know who'd—"

"It's got to be Miley." Her voice was tight and breathless, like his was, both of them sounding like someone who's just taken a blow to the stomach. "Who else could it be? He's the only one who knew…but how could he have known where she was? I didn't even know until you gave me that piece of paper—" Her face crumpled—for one brief moment—then settled into a mask of rigid control. She turned in a swift, unbalanced jerk and gripped the edge of the countertop to steady herself. "The paper—the one with her name and address—where is it? I put it down, right here. Did you see it? When we got home last night? It's not here. It's not *here,* Holt—"

"Miley must have found it when he broke in here yesterday," he said, more calmly than he felt. "Probably right after we left. He was looking for the money, you said. I guess he figured he'd found a way to get it out of you."

"This is my fault." She was pacing, hugging herself, her face still empty of all emotion. Only her eyes were alive, crackling with rage, and he understood now why she wore the sunglasses when she played cards. "I should never have asked you to find her. It was stupid. Why did I think I had anything to give her? It was selfish, that's what it was. Stupid and selfish. God, I can't even—"

"Cut it out. You may be the reason this happened, but it's hardly your *fault.* Look, there's one good thing, at least. He's not likely to hurt her, right?"

She stopped pacing to give him a hard look. Then she seemed to deflate as she sagged back against the counter. "I don't know. Miley's a weasel and a coward, but he's desperate. Plus, the people he owes money to probably wouldn't hesitate to hurt him and anybody else if it'll get them what they want. And like I told you—I can't get to the money. At least, I don't know how to get to it. It's in an 'irrevocable trust'—whatever that means."

"It means you can't get to it," Holt said grimly.

"Okay, so what should we do?" She seemed to vibrate with energy. He thought of a warrior, adrenaline-charged and primed for battle.

He picked up the remote and thumbed the television off. "The first thing we have to do is go to the police."

"Go to…the police." She said it the way someone would who hasn't had many reasons to be reassured by that prospect.

He took her gently by the arms. "Think, Billie. That cabdriver is going to do so for sure, the minute he sees that Amber Alert. If he hasn't already. I'm expecting to hear sirens any second."

She stared at him as if the words weren't making sense, and what he wanted to do more than anything in the world was pull her into his arms and just hold her for a while, until the shock of this had diminished, or at least let her know he was there to prop her up if she wanted to break down.

Fat chance of that, he thought. And anyway, there wasn't time. He planted a quick kiss on her forehead and was about to release her when the phone rang, making them both jump and clutch at each other.

She stared at it as she might a coiled rattler, then looked back at him with a question in her eyes. He nodded. She walked over to the counter, wiped her hands on her bare thighs and picked up the phone.

Her heart banged inside her chest like something trapped and trying desperately to get out. She tried to take a breath, but there was no place to put it, so she held it and managed a raspy, "Hello?"

When Billie heard the voice on the other end she almost dropped the phone. She wanted to hurl it through the window…pound it against something until it broke into a thousand pieces.

"Hey, Billie, you watchin' television? You seen that Amber Alert thing they got goin' right now?" The voice sounded high, excited. Scared.

He better be scared because I'm going to kill him, she thought.

Her rage-fogged vision cleared enough so that she could see Holt trying to get her attention, his eyebrows raised in a frowning question. She threw him a look and gave a jerky nod, and he mouthed the word *speaker.*

She jerked the phone away from her ear, but the buttons on it were shimmering and out of focus, and her hands were shaking too hard to do anything with them anyway. Holt took the instrument out of her hands, punched a button, and Miley's voice came slinking into the room.

"—you better turn it on. I'm not kiddin'—"

"I've seen it." She felt like flint, the stuff of ancient spears—brittle, hard, capable of killing. "If you hurt her—"

"Jeez, Billie! What kinda guy do you think I am? I'm not—"

"I know what kind of guy you are, Miley—the kind who'd do anything to save his own ass. And if you touch one hair on my daughter's head—"

"Hey. You got no room to threaten me. I'm holding the cards, here, not you. You give me what I want, I give her back to her parents, good as new. It's as simple as that."

Billie looked at Holt, then closed her eyes so he wouldn't see her fear. Her fingers tightened around the phone, which had grown slippery in her hand. "Look— I told you the truth, Miley. I don't have the money. I can't give you what I don't have."

"Hey…that's cool. You don't have the quarter mil anymore—I get it. So, you just have to win some more. I got the buy-in money and you're all signed up."

Her stomach went cold. "What are you talking about?"

"The tournament—at the Mirage. You're in. All you have to do is show up—and win, of course. You win the tournament, you give me what I need, the kid here goes home, and you get to take home what's left of the pot. Everybody wins."

"You are insane," she said, unable to keep her voice steady. "I haven't played a hand in more than three years. I'm out of practice. And what if the cards don't go my way? You can't seriously think—"

"You think I'm not serious?" His voice went shrill. "You think this isn't serious, what I'm doing here? This oughta show you how serious I am. This is my *life* I'm talkin' about. You better win, Billie. You hear me? You *better* win, and win big. Or else this kid isn't ever gonna see her mommy and daddy again."

"Miley, wait! At least tell me—"

But there was nothing but a dial tone. She let the

phone slip from her fingers and never even saw where it fell. Her knees buckled. She felt Holt's arms come around her and allowed herself to be held, and to hold on to him, for a moment. Just a moment. Then she pushed away from him, straightened and said hoarsely, "I'm okay. I'm okay."

He let her go. She turned in a lost sort of way and combed the fingers of both hands through her hair. Coughed, and threw him a fierce look. "So…I guess we really have to go to the cops, huh?"

"Yeah, we do. We're going to be their number-one suspects the minute that cabbie puts two and two together."

"What makes you think they're going to believe us?" she said in a bleak voice. "And if I'm in jail, how am I going to—"

"I thought about that, too. I think I know somebody who can help us."

"So, you still have friends in law enforcement?"

"You could say that." He gave her a dark smile. "Go get dressed so we can get out of here before the cops show up on your doorstep. I'll tell you about it on the way."

He waited until he heard her closet door slide back, then picked up the phone from the counter where she'd dropped it, hoping there was caller ID. There was. He hit the button for incoming calls, and at the same time he was opening and closing drawers, looking for pencil and paper. He found what he needed on the third try, scribbled down the number of the last call and tucked the paper in his shirt pocket. Then he took out his cell phone and scrolled down through his speed-dial list to the one he wanted.

A brusque voice answered on the second ring. "Portland P.D., Homicide, this is Detective Ochoa—can I help you?"

"Uh…yeah," Holt said, "I'm looking for Wade. He anywhere around, by any chance? This is a friend of his—Holt Kincaid—I think we met last spring, during that serial killer thing…"

"Holt Kincaid…oh, yeah—the P.I., right? Sure, I remember you. Wade's out of the office, but I'll tell him you called."

"He on a case?" Holt's hopes of help were sinking fast.

The Portland detective chuckled. "Nah…I think he went home to have lunch with his wife. You know how these newlyweds are. If you have his cell or home number, you might try him there."

"Thanks," Holt said, and disconnected. Letting out an impatient breath, he checked his speed dial again. This time he got voice mail.

"Hey, Wade, this is Holt Kincaid. Give me a call back on my cell when you get this message. Thanks." He hesitated, then added, "It's important."

He disconnected and was searching his phone book for more options when Billie came in looking flushed, tucking the tail of a black long-sleeved pullover shirt into the waistband of khaki cargo pants. She looked ready to take on the world, he thought. All she needed was a flak vest with big letters on the back that said SWAT.

"Ready?" She sounded out of breath.

"Yeah." He tucked his cell phone in his pocket, snatched up his jacket from the chair back he'd hung it on last night—a lifetime ago. "You happen to know where the police station is?"

Naturally, his cell phone rang on the way, and just as he was maneuvering through erratic lunch-hour traffic. He fumbled the phone out of his pocket and handed it to Billie.

"Here…I don't talk and drive. Tell him I'll be with him as soon as I find a place to park."

He heard her say, "Holt Kincaid's cell phone…" and then, "Yeah, he's right here. He just has to find a place to park. Hold on." She held the phone face down on her thigh. "He says it's Wade, returning your call."

"Yeah, I know." Muttering under his breath, Holt made a right turn down a side street and into the parking lot of an auto parts store. He pulled into an empty space and left the motor running. Billie handed him the phone.

"Hey, buddy," he said.

Wade's voice came back to him, sharp with suspicion. "Who was I just talking to?"

Holt said, "Uh…" and glanced over at Billie.

"You call me outta the blue, tell me to call you back, it's important. So I do, and a woman answers the phone. You found her, didn't you? Brooke told us you thought you might have. Tell me that wasn't my baby sister I was just talking to."

"Uh…" said Holt again, but this time at least he had the presence of mind not to look at Billie. "Yeah…and I'll tell you all about that later. Right now, though, we've got a bit of a situation. May have. I don't suppose you have any friends in the Las Vegas Police Department?"

"We?" Wade's tone was instantly serious. "Is my sister in trouble with the law? *Again?* My God, Kincaid, is this another situation like Brooke's?"

"No, no—nothing like that. At least…I hope not. May need you to put in a good word for us, though. If you wouldn't mind."

"Mind? Hell, I'll do better than that. I've got some personal time coming. How 'bout I see you there in… say, what?" There was some muffled mumbling, and then, in the kind of quiet voice he'd probably use to calm distraught witnesses: "Tee's already looking up flights. She says it's important, and you know I don't argue with her about things like that."

"Wade? If you wouldn't mind, it might be a good idea to bring her along, too."

Wade gave a snort of laughter. "You think she'd let me leave her behind? She's just reminded me we haven't really had a honeymoon yet, plus she's never been to Vegas. We're on our way, my friend. You just hang in there—and in the meantime, you take good care of my baby sister, you hear me?"

"I mean to," Holt said softly, and disconnected. He looked over at Billie and found her watching him, and for once he couldn't read her eyes. "What?" he said as he handed her the phone, more sharply than he meant.

Her gaze didn't waver. She took a quick little breath, hesitated another second, then said slowly, "I've just been remembering something. You told me one of my brothers is named Wade, and that he's a cop in Portland, Oregon. Tell me the truth, Kincaid. Was I just talking to my brother?"

"Yeah, you were." And because he suddenly realized his own emotions were piling up behind the dam of his self-control, and he for sure didn't want to deal with her family issues, he put the Mustang in Reverse and backed out of the parking space.

"And he knows it was me?"

"Yep."

"And he's coming to help us? Just…like that?"

"You're his sister," Holt said flatly, as the Mustang lurched out of the parking lot and back onto the street. "It's what families do. Help each other when they need it. Get used to it."

She didn't reply, and he drove for a good way in silence.

It wasn't until he was pulling into the parking lot at the police headquarters that it hit him. He gave a sharp bark of laughter, and Billie's head jerked toward him.

"I just thought of something," he said, grinning and slowly shaking his head. "You're not gonna believe this. This brother of yours. He's a police detective, right?" She nodded in puzzled agreement. "And guess what, his last name is *Callahan*."

She still looked uncomprehending, so he added in exasperation, "You said it—*Dirty Harry*, remember?"

She covered her eyes with one hand, laughing silently.

Billie had been in police stations before. Those past experiences had not been pleasant, and so far this one wasn't any better. She felt nervous and scared, for a lot of good reasons, but more than that, she felt *angry*. Betrayed. Those memories, those feelings...she thought she'd steered her life into a place where she'd never have to feel like that again. Yet, here she was. And she didn't know who to be mad at. Who to blame.

"I hate this," she whispered to Holt, and it seemed so natural now to tell him how she felt, although she'd never done that with anyone else before. "The way they look at you. They make me feel like I've done something bad even when I know I haven't."

"That just means you have a conscience."

He, at least, seemed unfazed by the fact that they'd been questioned, together and separately, for several hours. Meanwhile, Holt's Mustang and cell phone had been gone over with all the diligence the LVPD forensics teams could muster, and their identity documents checked and rechecked. Billie had even volunteered a sample of her DNA to corroborate her claim that she was the missing girl's biological mother. Which, as Holt had pointed out when she'd told him she was going to do it, could also work against her, since it would seem to give her a motive for kidnapping. Now they were together again, in a small, square room without windows, without much of anything in it except for a metal table and several hard chairs, and the single, unwavering eye of a video camera high in one corner.

"Do you think they believe us?"

"I think they'd like to." He was sitting relaxed in his chair, arms folded on his chest, and his eyes, resting on her, were calm. "Problem is, we're all they've got. And we're so perfect for it. Biological mom hires private investigator to find child she gave up for adoption, they go to see the kid, and the next day she's abducted? Doesn't get any more perfect than that." He smiled wryly. "Hell, I'm not even sure *I* believe us."

Her lips felt numb; she couldn't make herself smile back. "But…they'll check at the airport, won't they? They'll ask Tony. He'll tell them he brought us back here last night."

"Yes," Holt said gently, "and I'm sure they've already done that. Doesn't mean we—you—couldn't have hired somebody like Miley to kidnap your daughter."

She put a hand over her eyes and whispered, "Oh, God." After a moment she took her hand away and glared up at the video camera. "They're probably listening to us right now, aren't they?"

"Probably."

"They know I have a rap sheet, I guess…." Her stomach felt raw and sore, and there was a sick, sour taste in her mouth. "From when…I was on the street."

Yes...all the miserable, stupid things I did then, to stay alive. Panhandling, shoplifting, trespassing...but at least— She blurted it out. "I want you to know, I never did drugs. And I never turned tricks."

He sat up suddenly. Felt as if she'd slapped him. "My God—Billie..."

"You believe me, don't you?" She stared at him with hot, dry eyes.

The air between them was like a solid thing. He wanted to reach through it to touch her, but it seemed impenetrable. He said huskily, "I believe you. But it wouldn't matter to me if you had. I'd never judge you."

"Yeah, you would. And it would matter. You might not think so, but it would. You know why I didn't?" Her gaze didn't waver, just seemed to grow hotter and brighter—and at the same time more distant. Like stars. "I didn't because I figured if I was going to do that I might as well go back home. At least there I'd have food and a warm place to sleep."

What could he say? The effect of the words and that hot, hard gaze was enough to make him feel cold and shaky clear through to his insides. Staring back at her, he kept seeing all those battered young bodies he'd had to look at, in so many morgues, in so many cities, laid out cold and still with clean white sheets covering the evidence of how cruelly life had treated them. So many without names... All he could do was look at her and hope she'd understand his silence.

After the longest ten seconds he'd ever lived through, she sat back and exhaled sharply.

"Why are they still keeping us in here? They've asked us everything they possibly could. What are they waiting for?"

He cleared his throat. "Well, I think—" And just then the door opened to admit the Las Vegas detective they'd spent so much time with earlier in the day. Right behind him were the two people Holt wanted most in the whole wide world to see. "I think—" he finished, grinning as he rose to his feet "—for this."

As he went to greet his visitors, he caught a glimpse of a face gone white as chalk, and he knew then that what scared Billie Farrell—or Brenna Fallon—more than the entire Las Vegas Police Department combined was this moment, and what was about to take place. Meeting this man—Wade Callahan.

My brother.

She had no recollection of having risen to her feet, but she must have. Now she stood with her hands on the tabletop to steady herself and watched them come into the stark little room.

She saw him first—a tall man with broad shoulders and a slightly rumpled look, a face with a rock-solid jaw wearing a hint of beard shadow, close-cropped brown hair and heavily lashed eyes a deep, dark shade of blue. Right now those eyes were frowning and aimed straight at her, even while he was busy shaking Holt's hand and clapping him on the arm. Then he pushed past everyone else in the room, and tables and chairs, too, and she was swallowed up in the biggest, strongest hug she'd ever known.

Except, unbelievably, that big, strong body was shaking. She could feel the hard edge of his jaw pressed against her head, and her feet didn't touch the floor as he whispered, "Hey, baby sister. Nice to finally meet you. I'm your brother Wade."

She didn't dare speak. Didn't dare laugh, or even draw breath. She was so fragile, her self-control so tenuous, one word…just one sound…would smash it to pieces.

Then there was a sound, and she didn't break after all. A soft, almost comical, "Ahem…"

Wade released her with a shaken laugh. "Yeah…all right, I know. Sorry, Tee…" He turned to bring the other person, the woman, forward, although he kept Billie tucked in the curve of his arm. "Hey—I want you to meet my wife. This is Tierney. Tierney…this is my sister Bren—"

"It's Billie," Holt said, from somewhere nearby.

The woman was lovely, with tousled blond hair and clear, beautiful blue eyes, so different from her husband's indigo, and worlds apart from Holt's hot-cold steel. She had sun-kissed skin, a scattering of freckles and a warm and generous smile. Something about her made Billie think of flowers.

"Hi, Billie," the blond woman said softly, and held out her hands to take Billie's. "Friends and family usually call me Tee." Her hands felt warm…so warm, and Billie realized hers were like ice.

"You read people's emotions," she said gruffly. "Holt told me." She tried to smile. "Guess this must be pretty intense, huh?"

Tierney's smile blossomed. "Oh, don't worry—I can block most people's most of the time." She gave Billie's hands a reassuring squeeze. "Think how awful it would be if I didn't."

But her eyes held Billie's for a few moments longer, and…it was the oddest thing. She wasn't psychic, she was sure of it—at least, she'd never even thought of such a thing before—but suddenly there was a voice inside her head, a voice that wasn't really a *voice* at all, more of a feeling, impossible to describe. And in words that weren't exactly words, but so clear it seemed as if they were words, it was saying, *You're not alone…we love you. No matter what happens, we're here with you now.*

"So," Holt said, "here's what we want you to do."

They were in a small squad room now—Holt and Billie, Wade and Tierney, several members of the Las Vegas Police Department assigned to the kidnapping case, and a couple guys from the FBI. They were scattered among the several desks in the room, some peering at computer screens or talking quietly on telephones.

Holt was sitting on the edge of a desk and Billie was standing in front of him, straight and stiff as a mannequin. He had his hands on her arms, but it wasn't enough. He wanted her *in* his arms. Wanted to do whatever he needed to do to get that dazed, scared, brave, stoic, *frozen* look off her face.

"You just need to buy us some time, okay?"

He waited for her nod and a barely audible, "Yeah, sure."

"All you need to do is to show up for the tournament, hang in for as long as you can. Give us time to find where he's holding her."

Her eyes looked flat and hopeless. "How can you? How can they? He could be... She could be anywhere."

He lowered his voice to a murmur and tipped his head toward the detectives poring over their computers in the room behind him. "These guys know their stuff, and they haven't been sitting around on their asses. They have some leads—they're working on those now." She just looked at him, clearly unconvinced. He forced a smile. "Plus, you've got me. I find people, remember?"

"Kincaid." One of the LVPD detectives—Holt was pretty sure his name was Vogel—held up an arm and beckoned him over to the desk where he was hunched over an array of electronic equipment along with a tech guy and one of the FBI agents. "I think we're ready here."

"Yeah...coming." Holt slid his backside off the desk but kept one hand on Billie's shoulder as he guided her over to where the three men were waiting. Her shoulder felt small-boned and defenseless, and he had to remind himself she was anything but.

The techie was a slightly overweight guy with

thinning red hair cut short and flat on top. He looked about nineteen. He handed Billie a phone, and Vogel said, "Okay, what I want you to do is call this guy Miley Todd back at the number he called you from. That's this number right here." He smoothed a piece of paper on the desk with one hand, and Holt recognized the note he'd scrawled before leaving Billie's. "We know it's a cell phone," Vogel went on, "so we can't trace it. But what we can do is try and ID the tower the signal's coming from. Understand? That'll narrow our search area. So we need you to keep him talking as long as you can. Can you do that?"

She nodded, and Holt saw her throat move. He thought she looked scared to death.

"Tell him you need proof he's got Hannah," he said, drawing her eyes to him, putting all the strength and confidence he could muster into the look he gave her. "Tell him you need to know she's all right. Keep him on the line as long as possible."

She nodded again. The techie donned a pair of headphones and pointed to her. She took a breath, let it out and punched in the number. A moment later, everyone in the room could hear the *brrr* of the distant ring.

Once. Twice. Three times. Holt was willing to bet nobody in the room took a breath. Then there was a click, and a voice, high and scared and one he'd heard before, said, "Yeah—who's this?"

"It's me—Billie." Holt couldn't believe how calm she sounded. Angry, yeah, but definitely not scared.

Miley, on the other hand, was freaking out. Holt wouldn't have thought his voice could get any higher, but it must be hitting close to high C.

"Billie? What the hell! How'd you get this number?"

"Caller ID, you moron," Billie replied, and several people in the room had to stifle laughter.

"Hey, you better watch who you're callin' names, okay? I'm not kiddin' around here. You better not be talking to the cops, either, you hear me? Billie? You hear me? No cops!"

"Yeah—" she cleared her throat; her eyes were closed "—yes, all right. Just…calm down, okay? Look, I'm doing what you want, I'll be in the damn tournament when it starts tomorrow. I just want—" her eyes flicked to Holt's for one panic-stricken moment, then she caught a quick breath and rushed on "—I need to know she's okay."

"I told you, I'm not gonna hurt her. That's all you need to know."

"Yeah, but she's probably scared to death. Let me talk to her, okay? Just let me tell her—"

"Hey, I know what you're doing." His voice went up the scale again. "You're trying to keep me talking so you can trace this call. You better not be tryin' to trace this call, you hear me? Won't do you any good anyway, 'cause the kid's not here."

Billie's fingers were gripping the phone so hard her knuckles were white. "Where—"

"Yeah, right, like I'm gonna tell you? Somewhere

safe, is all you need to know. Somewhere you won't find her, neither, not without me. So you just better not be talkin' to the cops. Because if the cops do find me? If anything bad happens to me, you're never gonna find her. You hear me, Billie? Nobody's ever gonna see that little girl again."

Chapter 9

The weather turned warmer that evening. The wind had died down; the front, or whatever it was, had moved on east. This being the desert, the temperature had dropped with the coming of darkness, and Holt knew it would be chilly by morning, but for now it was pleasant enough that the tourists were out strolling the Strip in droves.

Billie and Holt had had dinner with Wade and Tierney, who had flipped a coin to decide which of the touristy mega-hotel/casinos they should stay in for their first trip to Vegas, and belated honeymoon to boot. The Venetian had won the toss. Holt and Billie had left the newlyweds waiting for their turn at a gondola ride and had driven back to Billie's in time to meet the police technician who'd be setting up a monitor on Billie's landline.

While Holt and the techie had their heads together over the electronics, Billie had wandered out onto the patio in the backyard. After seeing the techie—whose name was Riley—to his van and locking up the house, Holt found her there, sitting cross-legged on the deck beside the empty pool. She wasn't wearing a jacket, just the long-sleeved pullover she'd put on that noon after getting the phone call from Miley. Her SWAT outfit, he thought, smiling to himself. And at the same time his heart felt curiously heavy.

"Hey," he said, and she looked up at him, smiling just a little, but not saying anything.

"What are you doing out here in the dark?" he asked, although it wasn't really dark, with the light from the kitchen pouring through the windows and a three-quarter moon bright overhead. He sat down beside her, not cross-legged—his joints were no longer comfortable with such extremes—but with his feet dangling over the side of the pool.

She looked down at her linked hands. "Just…you know. Thinking about stuff."

"Yeah, well…I guess you've got a lot to think about."

She took in a breath and shook back her hair. Looked up at the night sky. "Actually, I was thinking about the Grand Canyon."

What could he say to that? Considering everything that had happened to her in the past day or so, it seemed…unexpected. To say the least. Finally, he just said, "Yeah?" hoping she'd explain.

Instead, she asked, "You ever been there?"

"Nope," he said. "How about you?"

She shook her head. "Always wanted to. I meant to. I mean, I think everybody should see it, don't you? It's one of the most amazing things on the planet, and it's right *there.* So close. And I've never been. Don't you think that's…I mean, it just seems *wrong.*" Her voice had an odd little vibration in it.

It awakened a corresponding hum in his own chest, and he started to tell her something, then realized just in time that what he'd been about to say was, "We'll go. When this is over. I'll take you." As if it was a given they'd be together then.

"How come you have a pool with no water in it?" he asked after a moment.

She gave a little half laugh, then shrugged. "I don't know, it just seems like too much trouble. I mean, my parents had one, and they were always needing to do something to it—clean it, disinfect it, strain stuff out of it, fix the filter, heater…I think it's kind of like owning a dog. You know? Ties you down."

It occurred to him that he did know. That he knew exactly what she meant, because he was the same. Hell, he didn't even have a potted plant. "You've got plants," he said. "Aren't they a lot of trouble, too?"

"Yeah, but if they die it's not a big deal, you just throw them away and get new ones." There was something defensive about the look she gave him. "Nobody cries for a plant."

"No strings," Holt said.

"Right." After a moment, she took in another of those breaths that seemed like a portent—as if she'd turned some sort of mental page. "I was just thinking…it would be kind of nice to have water in the pool right now. I sort of wish I did. It would be nice to just…drift in the water…in the dark. You know?"

"So you wouldn't have to think," Holt said softly, and she gave a light laugh and said, "Yeah…"

Then she looked at him, and the naked longing in her face made him inhale sharply. He wondered if it was really the pool she was talking about at all, or if it was the strings she missed. Or if he was only projecting his own loneliness onto her. Loneliness he hadn't even been aware of until now.

He cleared his throat and said carefully, "I don't have a pool, but a warm bath or shower sometimes works for me."

She shook her head, and he could see a wistful smile. "Not the shower. Showers always make me think—it's sort of like a brain lubricant for me."

"Bath, then." He got to his feet and held out a hand to her. "Come on—I'll run it for you. Got any bubbles?"

She was laughing when he pulled her up, but the laughter died quickly, and a second later she was in his arms. Not the way it had been with them before, with the chemistry and fireworks and pounding heartbeats, but quietly, gently, with her arms wrapped around his waist and her cheek resting against his chest. He held her that way for a while, until he felt a tremor run through her. And in that moment, and that small shudder, he knew he wanted it, too—the water in the pool, the potted plants, a dog, maybe…most of all, *this*. A woman to hold, to share the Grand Canyon with, to run a warm bath for. *No…not a woman. Just this one.*

"You're cold," he said with gravel in his throat. "Let's go inside."

What is this I'm feeling? Billie thought. *Not scared, not lost…but like I've been that, and then somebody came to find me and he's got his arm around me, and now it's almost as if I've never been anything but safe and warm. And most of all, not alone. I can barely remember what it felt like, all those years of being alone. As if they were a dream that's gone from your head when you open your eyes.*

But how can that be, when the truth is, this *is the dream, and one day soon I'll wake up and he will be gone…*

"I don't think I have any bubble bath," she said. "Would dish soap do?"

"I guess. It softens hands…" he intoned, and she stifled a laugh against his soft cotton shirt.

In the kitchen, she got the bottle of dish soap from under the sink while Holt locked the door and turned off the lights, and they walked down the hall without touching. In the bathroom, she turned on the light, then stood holding the bottle of soap while he turned on the water in the bathtub, tested the water temperature and put in the old-fashioned stopper. When he finally straightened and his eyes reached for her across the brightly lit room, her heart stumbled.

What do I do with a man like this? she wondered. *This man with his steely eyes and a face almost as hard, but with a mouth that hasn't forgotten how to smile and makes me forget everything, even who I am. This man who's as much a loner as I am, maybe more, and yet he's here, with me, in my bathroom, running me a bath as if I'm someone who needs caring for and he's someone who's used to caring. Where does a man like this learn about caring? Softness? Gentleness? Love? I had parents, at least for a while. And a sister. Who did you have, Holt Kincaid?*

Almost without knowing she did, she handed him the bottle of soap. He poured some into the thundering stream of water, and a few tiny, perfect bubbles flew upward and drifted toward the light.

"Okay," he said, setting the soap bottle on the edge of the tub, "that should do it. Unless you'd like some music?" She shook her head. His eyes blazed into hers, and they, far more than the steam rising from the filling tub, made the room suddenly feel like a summer night in the tropics. "Okay, then, I'll get out of your way...." He paused beside her, laid one hand gently on her shoulder and leaned down to touch a kiss to her forehead. And would have gone on by and left her there, except...

She caught him by the hand. "Stay," she said, and

though it was barely a whisper, it bore the weight of command.

He stood looking down at her, not smiling, and she was glad he didn't smile. It would have ruined it if he'd smiled, even a hint of one. But his eyes were somber, and blanketed with unspoken questions.

She tilted her head toward the tub, rapidly filling with bubbles, and murmured, "Here. With me. The tub's big enough." And now it was she who smiled. "That's one of the good things about buying an old house."

He still didn't say anything, but reached past her to turn off the light.

"Why—" she began, and felt his fingertips touch her lips.

"Shh," he whispered. "Wait a minute."

And even before he'd finished speaking, moonlight was already pouring into the room, replacing the harsh man-made illumination and cloaking everything in softness and mystery. She made a wordless sound of approval and her fingers found the buttons on his shirt.

"Better turn off the water," he murmured in her ear, "or we'll have a flood."

She nodded and turned to comply, and he took advantage of the moment to nudge off his shoes and put his gun in a safe place on top of the toilet tank. Then she was back, her movements fluid in the charcoal filter of moonlight. Her shirt was gone without her seeming to have touched it; less than a second later he felt her fingers on his skin, the buttons of his shirt already undone. Her bra was the stretchy sports bra type, and she divested herself of it with what seemed like sleight of hand—a flourish of raised arms, a little shake of her head, and her small, perfect breasts were unveiled like a marble statue in a moonlit garden.

He felt his pulse leap in his throat and reminded himself once again to shield. To slow the tempo of his desire. To find *her* beat. This was her music they were dancing to.

The cargo pants—and whatever was underneath—made a shushing sound as they fell. Naked and unself-conscious as a child in the half darkness, she reached for his arm and held it for support as she used the toe of one foot to push the pants off the other, taking the shoe with it. The same procedure with the other foot, an impatient kick that sent everything to some distant corner, and her hands were back on the waistband of his pants. Her nearness made his head swim.

And while there was no conscious seduction in the way she undressed both herself and him, at the same time it seemed to him an intensely *intimate* thing. This house, this room, this moment… This, he realized, was her place of mystery and privacy, and for some reason she'd invited him in. He understood that there was a kind of innocence in the way she offered, and that it wasn't about sex, at least not at this instant, but more about the sharing of her innermost self. He felt both humbled and incredibly blessed. *What,* he wondered, *could I have done to deserve such a gift?*

She took his hand and he held on to her while she stepped into the pile of foam, then she steadied him while he did the same. There was no sound except for the faint hissing of disturbed bubbles. Then he heard the sound of unspoken delight, an indrawn breath, as she lowered herself into the water. He slid down behind her, holding his own breath as the water level came near but didn't quite reach the edge of the tub. There was a loud gurgle as water rushed into the overflow outlet. He eased back against the end of the tub and pulled her onto his chest, and she put her foot over the hole to keep the water level from dropping. He wrapped his arms around her and settled his chin on her hair, and she sighed, then laughed low in her throat.

He concentrated on clouds drifting across blue autumn skies…sunlight sparkling on water…the swaying of eucalyptus branches outside his bedroom window far away in Laurel Canyon. Anything to keep his mind off the lithe, slippery body draped across his.

"How's that?" he asked carefully, trying not to jostle anything, and she replied softly, "Nice."

Then she was silent for a long time, so long he might have thought she'd gone to sleep, but for the rapid tap-tapping of her heart against his arm.

"Holt, I'm scared." She said it the way she might have said, "My back itches." *Please scratch it for me.*

She didn't add that unspoken request, but he knew the response she wanted from him at this moment was the same as if she had.

"About the tournament tomorrow?" Her head moved on his chest, nodding. "You'll be fine," he said. And because he knew she wouldn't be satisfied with the automatic pat on the head, he added, "You're very good—I've seen you play."

"I haven't played in a long time. I don't know the new faces."

He lazily scooped a handful of warm water and smoothed it over her thigh like oil. "All you have to do is—"

"—buy you some time. I know." She stirred restively, to his increasing discomfort. "But what if I can't? What if I go out tomorrow?"

"You won't."

"How can you say that? You saw me play one time. And I'm sorry, but you don't know diddly about poker."

"True. But," he added after a pause to think about it, "I'm a big fan of Kenny Rogers."

She squirmed again, trying to look up at him. "Kenny—"

"You know, the song…"

"Oh— 'The Gambler.' Right."

"What is it he says? To play your cards right all you need to know is when to hold and when to fold. Is he right?"

She gave one of her little whiskey laughs. "Uh…you do know he wasn't really talking about poker, right?"

Now it was his turn to shift position, trying to find a place for her that would still allow his brain to function.

When he had her more or less settled, he pressed his face into her hair, inhaled the sweetness of her scent, then murmured, "It's an analogy, sure. They keep cropping up, these poker analogies—did you ever notice that? Maybe because they're so perfect?"

She lay quiet, now, in his arms. "Life's just one big poker game?"

"Isn't it? Think about it. You don't get any say in what cards you're dealt, it's all about how you play your hand." He paused and wrapped his arms more tightly around her. "You have to know when to walk away, when to run. And you do. Don't you?"

"Seems to me," she said in a sad, quiet voice that wrung his heart, "I'm pretty good at running. Always have been."

"Maybe…" His hands wanted to stroke her again… caress her. This time he let them, and he said huskily, "But not this time."

Like a playful otter she turned in his arms, twisted around so she could look at him, and he took her face between his hands and held it while he looked into the shadows that hid her eyes. "Right now, when it counts, you're still at the table. You could have walked away, but you didn't. You stayed in the game."

The sound she made could have been a laugh or a sob; it was too dark to tell. He brought her face to his and kissed her. "That's all you have to do tomorrow, Billie –stay in the game. Make it to the next round. Okay? Win us another day."

He waited for her nod, but instead she slithered upward and kissed him, and went on kissing him while her legs adjusted themselves around him in the confines of the tub. He groaned, groping blindly for willpower in the exotic jungle his senses had made of his reason. Blessedly, he found it, but allowed himself to savor, just for a moment, the hot, tight feel of her body around him. When he eased her away from him, every nerve and muscle in his body echoed her squeal of protest.

"The water's getting cold and my backside's numb," he said in a whisper.

"Wuss," she murmured.

"And the condoms are in the other room."

"Oh—right."

Weakened by laughter and desire, he let her pull him to his feet. Then he took the towel she gave him and wrapped her in it and carried her to her bed.

It was different this time. Billie couldn't have put into words why, exactly, but it just was. Sure, there wasn't the newness, the first-time nervousness, the collision of conscience with need, but it was more than that. Of course, a lot had happened—was still happening—but it wasn't that, either. Something was different inside *her.*

The shape and taste of his mouth, the prickle of his beard-rough face on the palms of her hands, his hard, long body and big, gentle hands—these things she hadn't even known before yesterday. Yet, now she felt as if she'd always known them.

This morning I told him I wasn't a forever kind of

woman, yet now I keep hearing the word forever *whispered over and over inside my head like a bit of song that won't leave me alone.*

But he hasn't changed. He still is not a forever kind of man. So where does that leave me?

Vulnerable. I could get hurt.

"What?" he whispered, staring down at her face in the darkness, his chest gone tight with tenderness. His fingers were cradling her head, and his thumbs, caressing her cheeks, had felt wetness there. "Billie…what's wrong?"

"Wrong? Nothing's wrong…must've missed a spot with that towel," she said, and her laughter was languid and sweet, so he thought he must have been mistaken.

Except that, when he bent his head to kiss away the moisture, he found it tasted faintly salty, like tears.

The ballroom at the Mirage was a zoo, a seething hive of humanity with a noise-level approaching damage limits. *Where did all these people come from?* Billie wondered as she stood in the entrance to the ballroom, searching the crowd for familiar faces. In the years since she'd last played in a major tournament, the popularity of no-limit hold 'em appeared to have exploded.

Yes, but it's still the same game, she reminded herself. The most important thing to have in a tournament of this size was still self-discipline. That, and a lot of luck. Miley had taught her that much, at least. Right now, she knew, the field included a whole bunch of really terrible poker players, most of whom would be gone by the end of the night's play. Later, when the players had been winnowed down to the top few, skill would make a difference. But on the first day of a tournament this size, it was mostly about luck. And discipline.

Billie knew she'd need both to make it through to tomorrow's play.

Just buy us some time, Billie. Give us one more day.

"Hey—Billie Farrell, is that you?"

She turned to find the source of the voice, and it was a moment before she recognized one of the familiar faces on the tour. During play he'd be wearing a hooded sweatshirt and huge sunglasses. Without his disguise he looked deceptively young and harmless. "Hey," she said. "Yeah…it's me. Couldn't stay away."

"Well, welcome back—as long as you're not at my table. What number are you at?"

She checked the card in her hand. "Uh…twenty-six."

He flashed a grin. "Thank you, Lord. Well—see you later. If we're both still around." He touched her elbow and moved off into the crowd.

Well, here goes, Billie thought, and followed.

She found her table and took her place, nodding at the players already seated as she placed her backpack under her chair. In the backpack were a bottle of water, a can of high-energy drink, and several granola bars. She wouldn't be drinking much; bathroom breaks could be few and far between. If she lasted that long. Also in the backpack were her sunglasses. She took them out and put them on, then arranged her allotment of chips on the table in front of her.

The last few players took their seats. So did the dealer, blank-faced and anonymous. A loud buzzer sounded, and the noise in the ballroom died to a suspenseful murmur. The tournament had begun.

She watched two cards come slithering across the blue-green table toward her. She put her hand over them and tipped up the corners. Ace-queen, suited. She laid the cards flat and sat back in her chair, her face an impassive mask.

Not a bad way to begin, she thought.

"O—kay," Detective Vogel said, "this is the area we're lookin' at, right here." He thumped the map on which he'd just drawn a large circle with a red marking pen, then turned to his audience. This consisted of Holt, Wade, Tierney and a couple of the LVPD detectives. The rest of the team were busy on the computers, and the FBI guys had been keeping a low profile, letting LVPD take the lead in the case. "Here's I-15. The tower's just off the interstate. He had to be somewhere in this range."

"What the hell's out there?" one of the detectives asked.

"Uh…Arizona?" somebody said, and got a few snorts of laughter in response.

Somebody else said, "A whole lotta desert."

"Well, there's Valley of Fire State Park." This came from out in the middle of the squad room, where Sergeant Sanchez, the only woman on the team, had been staring intently at a computer monitor. She glanced up and added, "Google Maps," by way of an explanation.

"Valley of Fire? Never heard of it," Vogel said.

"Says here," Sanchez went on, reading from the monitor screen, "it's Nevada's oldest state park."

"Where are you gonna hide a kid in a state park? There's nothing out there." Vogel ran a hand over the gray stubble of his brush-cut hair, then aimed a question at the group at large. "How're we coming on the credit card records? Anybody? Jeez Louise…"

One of the other squad members picked up a stack of papers and waved them as he wove his way around the desks. "We're going over them now. So far the only thing we've got just verifies the general location. The guy got gas at a station off I-15, right around the time he made that call to Ms. Farrell."

"Would you mind if I take a look?" Holt asked quietly.

"Have at it," Vogel said, and the other detective handed over the printout with a shrug.

Holt scanned down the list, then went over it again, while the briefing went on, suggestions and questions and reports fading to background noise.

"Find something?" Wade asked in an undertone.

Holt looked up at him, frowning. "Maybe." He tilted the sheet so Wade could see it and pointed. "Look how many times he stopped for gas. Here, here and here."

He and Wade looked at each other, then at the rest of the group.

"Got something?" Vogel asked.

"I don't know," Holt replied. "Seems like he's using an awful lot of gas. What kind of vehicle burns that much gas? And might be found in a state park?"

"An RV," Vogel said, swearing under his breath.

There was a brief little silence, then everybody shifted into Drive at once. The room seemed to crackle and hum with activity, and Holt felt the excitement like a current of electricity under his skin.

Vogel was spouting orders in a rat-a-tat-tat voice, like an arcade popgun.

"Sanchez—find out if there's camping in that park. Everybody—find out whether the suspect has an RV registered to him. If not, find out if he's got any friends or relatives, neighbors who own an RV. Find out if there've been any reports of stolen RVs in the past forty-eight hours. Come on, people, let's go! Clock's ticking!"

It was late when Holt got back to Billie's place, but even so, he beat her there. He parked on the street and looked at the dark house and empty driveway and told himself that was a good sign, that it meant she hadn't gone out of the tournament yet. At least, he hoped that was what it meant.

He didn't have a key to her house, so he turned off the engine and headlights and settled down to wait.

It wasn't the first time he'd had to sit in his car and wait for someone to show up...for something to happen. He'd been doing stakeouts since his early years on the force. To pass the time back then, he'd think about the case in progress, go over every detail, much the same way he did now when he was battling imsomnia, only in his mind. This time, though, instead of cold facts and hard details, his mind kept filling up with images. Faces. Some of them were hazy and indistinct, some soft-edged, like old photographs. Some were painful, stark and vivid.

Brenna Fallon, fourteen years old, in a photograph with worn edges...

Gaunt faces, with empty eyes...the faces of homeless teenagers gathered under an overpass to keep out of the rain...

Billie sitting in the moonlight on the edge of an empty swimming pool, her face wistful as she talks about the Grand Canyon...

And not a face, but me, standing with my arms around her and my chin on her hair, looking in awe at the Grand Canyon...

My mother's face, not from memory, but from a photograph Aunt Louise had sitting on the piano...

Wade and Tierney, the way they look at each other...

Tony and Brooke. And what is it about the faces of people in love? Do I imagine it, or is there something that seems to shine from inside them, like a house with all the windows lit up?

He wasn't sure what woke him...hadn't been aware of falling asleep. He sat up straight and stared at the dark windows of Billie's house, and the cold seemed to seep into his bones. A cold that wasn't only from the temperature outside, which was definitely dropping, but also the chill of what he understood was loneliness.

He was staring at those dark windows when head-lights came sweeping across the white rail fence and the still, gray branches of the olive tree, and Billie's car pulled into the driveway.

She got out of her car and waited while he climbed out of the Mustang and walked up the driveway to meet her. The chilly desert night reached into the collar of his jacket and coiled around his ears, but he didn't feel it. She didn't say anything, just reached for his hand, and he walked with her along the pathway between the flowerpots. His heart was beating hard and fast, and he tried to think of what he could say to her to make her feel better. To let her know whatever happened, it wasn't her fault, and she hadn't failed.

They reached the bottom of the porch steps. She caught a quick breath and turned to him.

"I made it. Tomorrow…round two," she whispered, and came into his arms in a rush that left him without breath.

Chapter 10

"It'll be a lot different the second night of the tournament," Billie said. "Quieter."

"Hmm…" Holt's hand was stroking up and down her back, keeping a lazy rhythm with the slow up and down movement of his chest beneath her cheek.

Her eyelids drifted down, and she had to fight to make her lips form words. "There'll still be a crowd, just…most of 'em will be in the spectators' gallery. There'll be…I forget how many tables—around twenty, I think—each with nine players. The winner at each table advances to the next round."

"So," said Holt, "I guess there's twenty players left for that round. How many tables?"

She managed a feeble head-shake. "Four tables, usually. But that's when some of the big-name poker stars sit in, so it comes out to six players per table. And from that point on it'll probably be televised."

"And that's tomorrow night?"

"Yup. So…even if by some miracle I make it to the semi-final round, that's still only…"

"One more day." His chest lifted, then slowly settled with a long sigh. His arms tightened around her and she felt a stirring in her hair and then the warm press of his lips. "Give us that, love, and we'll find her."

"Promise?" she whispered, smiling because she knew how silly a thing it was to ask. And aching in her throat because he'd said the word *love* and she knew it didn't mean anything at all.

He responded, "Yeah, I promise." But of course it wasn't a sure bet and not even in his hands, so how could he make such a promise?

And yet…it was good to hear, and she felt her eyelids suddenly floating on a film of moisture she didn't understand at all. It couldn't possibly be tears, because for one thing, she never shed tears, wasn't even capable of it. And for another, what she was feeling right then was his nice, solid chest under her cheek and the steady thump of his heartbeat in her ear, and his arms strong and warm around her. So why would something so sweet and good and wonderful make her cry?

* * *

Holt left Billie sleeping and stole out of the house at zero-dark-thirty the next morning. He'd asked Billie for one more day, and he didn't want to waste a minute of it if he could help it. He picked up some fast-food drive-through breakfast biscuits and coffee and went straight on to police headquarters, figuring he'd be the only one of the team working the kidnapping in the squad room at that hour. Instead, he found Vogel and Sanchez and a couple of the others already there, sitting on desk corners scarfing down doughnuts and slurping coffee out of disposable cups. He handed around the sack of bacon-and-egg biscuits and helped himself to one before he picked a roosting spot on a desk opposite Vogel. He waited while the detective took a huge bite of his sandwich, chewed, then swallowed it down with coffee.

"Caught a break," Vogel said, waving what was left of the biscuit in its paper wrappings in the general direction of the rest of the squad. "Sanchez managed to track down a cousin of Todd's who says she loaned her RV to him the day before the kidnapping. Also gave us his current address." He took another bite. "Evidently, he's been bunking with his girlfriend. This cousin said he and the lady showed up asking if they could borrow the RV because they wanted to 'go camping.'"

"You've been busy," Holt said, sounding a lot calmer than he felt.

Vogel nodded as he chewed. "We got a unit sitting on the girlfriend's place. Car in the driveway, no sign of the RV."

Holt drank coffee and cleared his throat. "You figure one's holed up there and the other's staying with the kid in the RV?"

Again Vogel nodded. "According to what Todd told your friend Billie, finding him isn't going to get us the kid, so my guess would be the girlfriend drew the short straw. Anyway, we don't want to move on the girlfriend's place until we know more about who's where. What we really need is to find that RV." He nodded toward the big screen in the front of the squad room. "Question is, how? It's gonna be like looking for the proverbial needle in all that."

Holt stared at the screen with narrowed eyes. He assumed what he was looking at were satellite photos of the search area. The Valley of Fire. A turbulent sea of red and gold, carved by wind and water over millions of years. Incredibly beautiful, but desolate. And vast.

"We'll have eyes in the air at first light—" Vogel looked at his watch "—right about now, actually. But even with choppers and planes, it could take days. There must be a million places out there to hide an RV. And God knows how many RVs are out there right now. How the hell are we gonna know if it's the right one?"

"I think I might know somebody who can help with that," Holt said, reaching in his pocket for his cell phone.

Opened it, found his batteries were on life support, shoved it back in his pocket and frowned at the room. "Anybody know the number for the Venetian?"

Vogel gave him a skeptical look. "You're thinking the *psychic?* Even if I believed that stuff—and I'm not sayin' I do or I don't—how's she gonna help?"

"She's an empath—picks up on emotions. Figured maybe if she got close enough, she might be able to home in on the vibes of a scared little girl." Holt gave an offhand shrug and downed the last of his coffee. He wasn't about to waste breath trying to convince somebody of something he'd seen proof of with his own eyes. Something like that you either believed or you didn't. "Figured it couldn't hurt, right?"

Vogel stared at him for a moment, then tossed his empty coffee cup in the general direction of a trash can and pointed at his squad as he slid off his desk perch. "Sanchez—get me the Ven—"

"Already on it," Sanchez drawled, cradling a phone next to her ear.

"Got another phone I can use?" Holt sent his trash after Vogel's. "My cell phone's…"

"Sure—use that one right there." The detective was already halfway across the room, yelling at somebody else. "Hey, Turley, those choppers in the air yet? Get me the tower out at—"

Holt picked up the phone on the desk behind him and tucked it under his jaw while he took out his cell phone again and found the number he wanted in his phonebook. He put away the cell phone and punched in the number. After a couple of rings a sleepy voice answered.

"This better be Publishers Clearing House…"

"Tony, it's me," Holt said, then listened to some swearing. "Look, you know I wouldn't call this early if it wasn't important. Where are you? How soon can you get back to Vegas?"

"Never left," Tony said, in the middle of a huge yawn. "Brooke's on her way here. You didn't think she was gonna stay away once I e-mailed her those pictures I took—you kiddin' me?"

Somebody was definitely on his side, Holt figured. He let out a breath. "Man, you don't know how glad I am to hear that. Need another favor, my friend. Listen, will that toy of yours carry three passengers?"

"Three? Sure, if I leave my cameras, and if two of you don't mind sitting on the floor."

"Okay," Holt said, "get your gear and meet us at the airstrip. Can you be there in an hour?"

Billie woke up and knew before she opened her eyes that it was later than she'd ever slept before. A sickening lurch in her stomach reminded her she'd not only overslept, she'd also failed to show up for work.

Too late to worry about that now.

For a few more minutes she lay in her bed, listening to the silence of an empty house. Wondering why she'd never noticed before that the silence had a weighted, suspenseful quality, as if the house itself was holding its breath, waiting for something to come and fill the void. A voice, a laugh, a country song playing on a radio, the morning news on television, the tinkle of silverware on plates...

She got up, pulled a T-shirt on and wandered out to the kitchen, where she found the light blinking on her message machine. Three messages, the digital readout on the police recorder said. She punched the button, heard two hang-ups, then Holt's voice.

"Mornin', sunshine. Don't worry about going in to work. I called your boss. In case he asks, you're having stomach problems. I figured that covers a lot of territory, so you can fill in the blanks however you want to. So...rest up, whatever you need to do, for...you know, tonight. I don't know if I'm supposed to wish you luck, or not. So...break a leg, or whatever you say in the world of professional poker. Just hang in there, darlin'. And...I'll call you later. Okay...'bye."

She stood for a moment, her finger poised to play the message again, just to hear his voice. Told herself that was stupid, and went to make coffee instead. She was measuring coffee into the basket when the phone rang, making her jump so that the grounds went all over the countertop instead. She wiped most of them into the sink, brushed her hand off on the front of her T-shirt and picked up the phone, her heart already lifting into a quicker, more hopeful cadence, knowing it must be Holt, calling her back as he'd said he would.

"Hey," she said with a softness in her voice she hadn't even known would be there.

"Where you been? I been callin' you all morning."

Cold rage washed over her. She wrapped her arms across herself and shivered. "Miley."

"Yeah, it's me—who did you think? So, you did it, didn't you? Went to the cops. I told you—"

"Don't be stupid. The cops, the FBI—they're all over it without any help from me. What did you think was going to happen? You grab a little girl off the street and her parents aren't going to notice? Jeez, Miley, what were you thinking?"

"I told you what I'm thinking. You just need to win that tournament and everything's gonna be okay. I know you made it to the second round, so that's good. You just keep winning and everything's gonna work out."

"Miley, you know what the odds are of winning that tournament? Even if I was the best player in the world—"

"You just better be the best. You hear me?" His voice turned menacing. "You better win, Billie."

There was a click, and then nothing. Billie looked over at the recorder the police technician had set up, but it had nothing to tell her, either. She carefully returned the phone to its cradle and pressed her knotted fist against the cold flutter in her belly. *Stomach trouble—yeah, right.*

Find her, Kincaid. Please…find her.

* * *

Holt shifted, trying to find relief for his backside without taking his eyes off the tapestry of red, purple and gold unfurling beneath him. On the other side of the plane, Wade was sitting facing backward with one knee drawn up, the other stretched out in front of him, face pressed against the window. In the front seats, Tierney and Tony were also staring down at the incredible desert-scape known as the Valley of Fire. Aptly named, Holt thought, especially considering whoever had come up with the name probably hadn't had the opportunity to see it from the air, with the sun low in the sky, painting parts of the incredible rock and sandstone formations with scarlet and gold and casting others into purple-and-indigo shadow. He'd heard Tony cussing a few times, bewailing the absence of his cameras, but it had been a long time now since any of them had said anything.

They were running out of time. Out of daylight, and out of time. The odds against Billie making it to tomorrow night's final table were…what? A thousand to one? He was no math wizard, but it had to be huge.

Hang in there, love…

But under that thought, his emotions were so much more. More raw, more complex. He didn't realize how much more, until Tierney threw him a quick glance and he saw how haggard and strained her face was.

"Sorry," he said softly, and she smiled.

Wade looked up at his wife. "How're you holding up, babe?"

Her smile wavered, but she murmured, "I'm fine."

"Anything?" Wade asked.

She shook her head. She'd reported some interesting pickups over the course of the long afternoon, so they knew what they were trying to do was possible, at least. But so far, nothing that might have been the emotions of a frightened little girl.

"We're losing the light," Tony said, telling them all what they already knew. The canyons below were more purple now than gold.

Holt watched the Cherokee's tiny shadow undulate across the landscape, playing hide-and-seek with the shadows. Then watched it fade and disappear as the sun sank below the horizon. He strained to see a pinprick of light, but there was nothing but deepening darkness. It occurred to him it was like a vast ocean of sand and rock, and they were looking for a single tiny lifeboat.

"Let's try one more pass," he said. "A little bit more to the north this time."

The plane droned on toward the north, and the silence inside the plane grew heavier. When the left wingtip dipped into a sharp bank, Holt's heart sank with it.

"Gotta call it a day, folks—sorry," Tony said. "Running low on fuel."

"That's okay, buddy, you did—" Holt got that far and was interrupted by a sharp gasp.

"Wait! Wait—go back!" Tierney turned to them, her face rapt, her blue eyes bright. She put her hand up to cover her mouth, because she was laughing along with the tears.

The accountant from New Jersey went all-in on a straight draw that didn't come through for him, and Billie's table was down to three—Billie, an Internet player from New Zealand who looked about fifteen and a middle-aged guy wearing several gold chains, who chewed constantly on a toothpick and kept staring at Billie's cleavage. Which was actually okay with her, since she'd gone to some trouble to produce the cleavage by means of an extremely uncomfortable push-up bra she'd bought in a moment of insanity and she almost never wore.

Most of the other tables were done, or down to their last two players. Billie had been playing conservatively, biding her time, trying to hold on as long as possible. But inevitably, her pile of chips had shrunk, and it was clear her two remaining opponents were running equally low on patience. The looks Toothpick Guy sent her now were more annoyed than lascivious.

On the next hand, Billie drew pocket tens. The wonder kid from New Zealand, the chip leader, folded. Toothpick Guy checked, but looked a little too smug about it. Billie checked, too.

The Flop was ten, deuce, three. Billie stared at the cards, confident her glasses would keep her eyes from betraying her. She waited as long as she could get away with, then bet a thousand. Toothpick Guy promptly saw her bet. Exuding confidence, but not too much.

The Turn card shot onto the table. Another deuce. Again Billie stalled. A full house wasn't a sure thing, but she was almost out of chips. This hand was probably as good as it was going to get, and besides, what choice did she really have?

She went all-in.

Toothpick Guy's smug smile faded when he saw her full house. He had pocket queens, both red. Two pair, queen high.

Time really did seem to stand still. She knew she was holding her breath, and even her heartbeat seemed to have been suspended.

In slow motion, the dealer dealt the final card—The River. It was the queen of spades.

Toothpick Guy let out a gusty breath and leaped from his chair, hands clapped to the sides of his head in joy and relief. Billie sat motionless.

It's over.

There was a shimmery noise inside her head that blocked out all other sounds: Her own voice saying the right things as she rose from the table and extended her hand to the two surviving players. The New Zealander, saying something sympathetic to go along with his rather sweet smile. Toothpick Guy, all teeth and graciousness now that he'd won. She felt people patting her on the back as she turned, no doubt wishing her well, and she didn't hear that, either.

I failed, Holt. I couldn't do it. Hannah Grace, I'm sorry. I'm so sorry...

Blind and deaf, somehow she wove her way through the ballroom—through the casino, through the rows of slots with their garish lights and dinging bells and avid, oblivious worshipers...through the vast and crowded lobby, noisy with people enjoying the glitz, glamour and excitement of Vegas. Cold air slapped her in the face, and she came to with a start, realizing she was on the sidewalk apron just outside the main entrance, under the portico where limos and taxicabs deliver their passengers. She hesitated, shivering, then began walking rapidly, not knowing or caring where she was going.

"Billie!"

Somewhere, lost in the shimmering noise inside her head, she heard someone calling. Calling her? Or was it her imagination? Didn't matter, she didn't want to talk to anyone, or see anyone. She kept walking.

"Billie—wait!"

That voice. The voice she'd been both hoping and dreading to hear. She turned, quaking inside, holding on to her self-control by a gossamer thread. And saw Holt farther down the drive, making his way toward her, dodging around people, pushing past some. She started toward him, then halted, unable to make her legs take another step.

Then he was there, reaching for her, but she put out her hand to stop him from pulling her into his arms.

"I'm out," she said, words coming rapidly in a hoarse

voice, blunt and unforgiving. "I couldn't do it. I tried, but I lost. I didn't—"

"Billie—listen to me." He was shaking his head, gripping her arms. And smiling.

None of that registered. "I'm sorry, Kincaid. I couldn't—"

He gave her a little shake. "Billie, it doesn't matter. Don't you understand? It's okay. We've got her."

In that instant, time and space did strange and impossible things. Time stopped. The universe shrank down to the tiny space that included only herself and the man holding on to her...holding her up...holding her together. She stared at him and heard a distant voice asking, "She's okay?"

And Holt's lips moved and formed the words, "Yeah...she's okay. She's with her parents. Hannah's fine, Billie. She's fine."

The bubble popped. Sound rushed in. Sound and movement and thought. "What about Miley?" she asked. "Did they get him?"

"He's in custody."

"What's going to happen to him?"

She asked it in a hard voice, but there was something about the way she held herself... Holt stared down at her dark lenses, reflecting bits of light from the neon circus of the Strip, then reached up and gently took them off. Her eyes gazed back at him, dark and defensive, and he marveled that someone with a heart so battered and bruised could still find room in it for a rat like Miley Todd.

"You care about him," he said softly.

She hitched a shoulder. "I don't want—I mean, he did save my life."

Holt slipped an arm around her and tucked her against him as he started walking along the hotel drive. "I think the guy was actually glad to see the cops show up. Probably thinking, better them than the guys he owed money to. Anyway, he's probably going to be talking to the feds about witness protection in exchange for telling them about the guys he was in hock to. Turns out they're part of a pretty big organized crime syndicate the feds have been trying to bring down for a long time. Don't worry about Miley Todd—I have a feeling he's going to land on his feet."

She drew a long, shaky breath. "I can't believe it's all turned out okay." She hesitated, then craned to look at him. "She's really all right? She must have been so scared. You're sure—"

"See for yourself." And while she stared at him uncomprehendingly, he lifted his arm and signaled to the LVPD squad car parked in a fire lane a little farther along the drive. The car door opened. "Billie," he said gently, "there's someone here I think you should meet."

Billie froze, seemed to become rooted to the concrete sidewalk. "No." Her voice was a terrified whisper. "No, no—I can't…"

A little girl was getting out of the squad car, still clutching the teddy bear they'd given her at the police station while they were waiting for her parents to arrive.

Billie was silent, although he could feel her shaking. She lifted a hand and pressed her fingertips to her lips.

He watched the girl's parents get out of the car. These were two very decent, ordinary people—not young and a little dowdy, maybe—the kind of people you'd expect to find at PTA meetings and on the sidelines at soccer games. The mom first—and she was the kind of mom you'd feel good about coming home to if you were a kid, Holt thought, because you'd know there was going to be something good to eat waiting for you in the kitchen, and a hug to go with it. Then the dad—the kind of dad you knew would be there to catch your bicycle when it wobbled, and who would tell you no when you asked if you could do something you knew in your heart was stupid and dangerous. The kind of people his own parents could have been. Would have been.

"They must hate me so much," Billie whispered.

He looked down at her and smiled. "I don't think these people are capable of hating."

But she went on standing there, looking at the couple standing with their hands on their daughter's shoulders, both protecting and encouraging. She seemed incapable of taking a step. She looked up at Holt, and the longing in her eyes squeezed his heart.

He gave her a nudge and, in a gruff-sounding voice he didn't entirely trust, said, "Go on—go meet your daughter."

Still she hesitated. "She…she knows who I am?"

He nodded. "Her mom said she's been asking about her birth mother. She wants to meet you."

"And…it's okay with them? Her mom and dad?" She sounded both disbelieving and hopeful.

"Yes," he said softly, "it's okay."

He took her hand, then, as if she were a child afraid of the dark. Guided her a few steps closer to the three people waiting beside the police car, then experimentally let go of her hand. She looked up at him and he smiled and nodded, then watched her walk on alone to meet her daughter. His face felt stiff, his throat tight and achy, and he folded his arms and straightened, making himself taller, sturdier, as if that would make him feel less alone.

Then he wasn't alone, as Wade came from one side to clap a firm hand on his shoulder, Tierney from the other to slip her arm around his waist.

"Look at her—not a tear," Wade said. He nodded toward his wife, who was openly weeping. "Tee's a basket case."

"Billie doesn't cry," Holt said. His arm was around Tierney's shoulders, and he gave her a squeeze. "Hey, I thought you could block."

She sniffled happily. "Who wants to block emotions like these? They're the good stuff. They feed my soul."

Holt didn't answer her; he never got the chance. Because just then two things happened, almost simultaneously.

A taxicab came barreling up the drive and zipped into

the space just ahead of the police car and right next to Billie and the Bachman family.

And Tierney stiffened, clapped a hand over her mouth and whispered, "Oh, God."

Instantly concerned for his wife, Wade said, "You okay, babe? What's wrong?"

"Nothing. Nothing's wrong," she replied, laughing as new tears slid down her already wet cheeks. "Wait— just wait."

The taxi's back door flew open and a woman climbed out—a tall, blond, beautiful woman—followed closely by Tony Whitehall. Billie looked up and turned to face the newcomers, her face frozen in a puzzled frown. And Holt felt as if he was watching a tableau, all its players poised in the moment just before the scene's dramatic climax.

Then…there was sound, and motion.

Brooke Fallon Grant marched up to her twin sister and said furiously, "Well, dammit, Brenna, you wouldn't come home, so I've come to get you!"

And Holt watched in shock as Billie—or Brenna— burst into tears.

The tidal wave of emotion that swept over him then was more than he knew what to do with—and definitely more than he wanted anyone to witness. He spun around, hands lifted, chest heaving, searching blindly for a private place, a hole to crawl into, a shelter where he could be alone and find a way to deal with the upheaval within him. But instead of aloneness, once again he found himself surrounded, arms wrapped around him, a strong hand gripping his shoulder.

"It's okay," Tierney whispered, hugging him tightly. "It's beautiful, isn't it? That's *family*."

And Wade said brusquely, "Well, Holt, my friend, looks like your job here is done." He paused while Holt coughed, cleared his throat, looked up at the lights and tried to laugh. "Have you told Cory and Sam yet?"

"Ah," Holt said, and cleared his throat some more. "Got a call in to them. Expect they'll be here soon." He hauled in a chestful of air and wondered why the achievement of something he'd been working toward for so many months didn't make him feel happier.

Tony came wandering up just then, his pit-bull face looking like it didn't know whether to laugh or cry. He shook Wade's hand with the two-handed grip that passed for hugging between guys, nodded toward Holt, sniffed and said, "Boy...this is something else, huh?" Then the three men stood silently and a little apart, arms folded on their chests, watching the two sisters. The two women had their arms around each other, heads close together, laughing, nodding, wiping eyes, laughing again...crying.

Tierney moved to stand close to Holt's side, and he thought it was strange that he didn't feel any need to widen the distance between them. There was something about her that he found comforting. Maybe, he thought, because he knew he couldn't hide his feelings from her anyway, so why worry about it.

"Does she know how you feel about her?" she asked quietly after a while.

He gave a soft huff of laughter. "No, I'm sure she doesn't. And I intend to keep it that way."

"Why?" She waited for him to answer, and when he didn't, she said, "If it makes a difference, she loves you, too." He still didn't reply, and he heard a sharp little intake of breath. "But it isn't that, is it? I think…for you that almost makes it…harder."

When she paused, his mind flashed back to the night before, in Billie's bathtub, with her all slippery and weightless on his chest, the weight all inside, where his heart should be.

Life's just one big poker game…

You don't get any say in what cards you're dealt, it's all about how you play your hand.

You have to know when to walk away, when to run.

"It's too big a gamble for you, isn't it? Loving someone…"

He threw her a look he knew she didn't deserve—hard and mean and born out of the darkness he could feel starting to close in around him. "If you mean, am I willing to risk losing somebody I love, the way I lost my parents—yeah, it's too big a gamble." *I can't do it. It just hurts too much.*

"Oh, Holt, this is *Vegas,*" Tierney said, and her voice was tender—not only the voice he heard with his ears, but the one he *felt,* deep inside his mind. "Don't you know…the greater the risk, the greater the reward? And sometimes the reward far outweighs the risk."

He could only shake his head, unable to speak.

Just then Billie looked up. Still flanked by and holding on tightly to her sister, she lifted her head and looked straight at him, and her tear-streaked face broke into a radiant smile. It was simply the most beautiful thing he'd ever seen in his life, more beautiful than any sunrise. Could even the Grand Canyon be more amazing?

If I could just wake up to that smile every day, he thought, it might be worth the risk…

What the hell. He held out his hand and she let go of her sister and came to him in a blind rush. He wrapped his arms around her and pressed his face into her hair…took a deep breath, closed his eyes…and went all-in.

Epilogue

"Pearse, could there *be* a more perfect day for a wedding?"

This was, of course, a rhetorical question, which Sam's husband knew better than to answer. He smiled at her, and she settled back in her folding chair as she added with a sigh, "Or a more perfect spot for one. This was a brilliant idea, havin' it in the Portland Rose Garden. I've got to hand it to Wade and Tee for comin' up with it."

"It was a good choice," Cory agreed. "A good compromise."

Sam snorted. "What compromise? The brides' hometown down in Texas has bad memories for both Brooke and Billie—I'm never gonna be able to call her Brenna,

Pearse, I'm sorry—and Las Vegas just seems a little bit tacky, if you know what I mean. So where were they gonna go? I think this is perfect. Not only is it the most gorgeous place I've ever seen, but it's where it all started, sort of." She knew she was chattering, but couldn't seem to help it. Her emotions were all over the place these days. "Well, not where it *started,* I suppose that would've been back home at Mama's house in Georgia, but it's where you first laid eyes on Wade. He was the first brother you found, and you first met him right here in this rose garden. And now…here we all are. Together."

She reached over and took her husband's hand and squeezed it, then sniffed. "Tell me the truth, Pearse—did you really think this day would come?"

Cory lifted her hand to his lips. "Never doubted it."

"Oh, come on, Pearse, don't lie to me. Don't you sit there and tell me there weren't a few bad moments. Like right here in Portland, when Wade mistook you for a serial killer and almost shot you?"

Cory rubbed ruefully at the back of his neck. "Yeah, that was a bad moment, all right. Especially when the real killer took that opportunity to take Tee hostage, and then shot Wade. For a while there I thought I'd found him only to lose him for good."

"And," Sam pressed on, "how about that day in the Kern River Canyon, when that woman almost ran us off the road, trying to kill Matt—"

"But she didn't," Cory pointed out, "and as a result, he and Alex found each other again."

"Finding your little brother in a wheelchair," Sam said softly. "That wasn't your best moment, either, Pearse."

"No…" He took a breath and smiled. "But that little brother of mine has taught me an awful lot about courage and inner strength. Like you did, Sammie June."

She nodded, and for a moment was silent. A soft breeze stirred through the evergreens that encompassed the rose garden and carried the sweet scent of the blossoms with it. Recorded chamber music floated on the warm spring air and the sun was gentle on her skin. Everything was beautiful, and in spite of that, she shivered.

"I don't know, though…I don't think anything your brothers put us through could hold a candle to your sisters. My lands, Pearse—when I think Brooke might have gone to prison—or worse—for murdering her ex-husband, when she was totally innocent…."

"I know. Thank God for Tony. And Holt. None of it would have happened without him."

She couldn't help but notice her husband's voice was husky, too. Weddings have a way of doing that, Sam thought.

She sat up straight. "Look—here they come. It's starting."

The men were coming along the pathway between rose beds flush with their spring bloom. The minister, first, wearing cream-colored robes. Then both grooms—Holt tall, straight and solemn, sunlight glinting off the silver at his temples…Tony a bit shorter and broader, solid as a mountain, his beautifully rugged face split in an irrepressible grin. Right beside him was Brooke's son, Daniel—such a handsome boy, so tall and blond, like his mama—looking up at the man who was about to become his new daddy as if the sun rose and set at his say-so. Then Matt in his wheelchair and Wade right behind him, both brothers handsome as sin. *Like their brother,* Sam thought with a misty glance at her husband.

The music rose in volume and quickened in tempo, and there was a rustling among the assembled guests as most of them turned to watch for the arrival of the bridal party. It was a small group, most of Sam's family having decided to wait for the big reception they were planning to throw for the happy couples back in Georgia. The whole staff of Penny Tours, Matt and Alex's river-rafting company, had driven up from California together in one of the company vans, and of course quite a few of Wade's fellow cops from the Portland P.D. were there in their dress uniforms. Most of the rest of the crowd consisted of Tony's family— his mom and sisters and kids, the husbands and brothers standing in back of the rest since they'd run out of folding chairs.

Then…the first of the brides' attendants started down the aisle. *So beautiful,* Sam thought, and felt a fluttering in her chest as she watched the little girl float toward her, carrying her basket of roses and wearing a simple ankle-length white dress. Hannah Grace waved shyly at her mom and dad, who smiled and waved back from their seats in the front row across from Sam and Cory.

Then it was Alex's turn, and she was grinning at the bunch from Penny Tours as if to say, *Hey, look at me, I'm wearing a dress!* Then Tierney, radiantly, gloriously pregnant, with eyes only for Wade, already teary-eyed from what Sam guessed must be an overwhelming banquet of emotions.

The music paused...a hush fell over the assembly, and over the gardens beyond. Then there was a collective sigh of breath as Brooke and Billie came from opposite sides of the garden to meet at the back of the aisle. They looked at each other, and Brooke lifted a hand to brush something from her twin sister's cheek. Then they both laughed, and turned...and waited.

Cory squeezed Sam's hand as he rose from his seat and went to meet them. He kissed each of his sisters on the cheek, then each one took an elbow, and they started up the aisle together.

Oh, Lord, that's done it, Sam thought. She clapped a hand over her mouth, but tears were already welling up and spilling over, and she didn't have a tissue, of course, to save her life. She watched through a blur as Cory handed over the brides to their respective grooms, then came back to take his seat. He handed her a handkerchief as he settled into the chair beside her, waited for her to mop her cheeks and blow her nose, then reached over and took her hand.

"Thanks," she whispered soggily. She leaned her

head on his shoulder. "Oh, Pearse, look at them up there. All of them together…did you ever imagine anything like this?"

Cory's laugh sounded wistful. "To tell you the truth," he whispered back, "I always imagined them the way I saw them last. You know—little. Just babies."

Sam drew a long breath, gathering courage. "Well, darlin', it sure does look like there's about to be a baby boom in your family. You don't look out, your family's apt to be as big as mine."

Her husband laughed without sound. "I don't think there's much danger of that—the Starrs have a pretty good headstart."

Another breath she didn't really need. "And…they're about to get bigger, too. By at least one."

He threw her an interested smile, eyebrows raised. "Really? Who's pregnant this time?"

"Oh, for Lord's sake, Pearse!" She glared at him in exasperation. And watched his face go blank, then pale with shock.

"Samantha?"

"Yes?"

"Sam—when did you? When were you…? And you're telling me this *now?*"

"It seemed like a good time."

"Does this mean—are you quitting the CIA? Are you going to quit flying? What—"

"Well, now, we'll cross that bridge when we come to it," she said serenely.

"Sam, when—"

She squeezed his arm and nodded toward the gazebo. "Hush up, Pearse. It's beginning."

* * * * *

*Celebrate 60 years of pure reading pleasure
with Harlequin®!*

*Harlequin Presents® is proud to introduce its
gripping new miniseries,*
THE ROYAL HOUSE OF KAREDES.
*An exquisite coronation diamond, split as a symbol of
a warring royal family's feud, is missing! But
whoever reunites the diamond halves will rule all....*

*Welcome to eight brand-new titles that unfold to
reveal the stories of kings and queens, princes and
princesses torn apart by pride and power, but finally
reunited by love.*

Step into the world of Karedes with
BILLIONAIRE PRINCE, PREGNANT MISTRESS
*Available July 2009
from Harlequin Presents®.*

ALEXANDROS KAREDES, SNOW DUSTING the shoulders of his leather jacket and glittering like jewels in his dark hair, stood at the door. Maria felt the blood drain from her head.

"Good evening, Ms. Santos."

His voice was as she remembered it. Deep. Husky. Perfect English, but with the faintest hint of a Greek accent. And cold, as cold as it had been that awful morning she would never forget, when he'd accused her of horrible things, called her terrible names....

"Aren't you going to ask me in?"

She fought for composure. Last time they'd faced each other, they'd been on his turf. Now they were on hers. She was in command here, and that meant everything.

"There's a sign on the door downstairs," she said, her tone every bit as frigid as his. "It says, 'No soliciting or vagrants.'"

His lips drew back in a wolfish grin. "Very amusing."

"What do you want, Prince Alexandros?"

A tight smile eased across his mouth and it killed her that even now, knowing he was a vicious, arrogant man, she couldn't help but notice what a handsome mouth it was. Chiseled. Generous. Beautiful, like the rest of him, which made him living proof that beauty could, indeed, be only skin deep.

"Such formality, Maria. You were hardly so proper the last time we were together."

She knew his choice of words was deliberate. She felt her face heat; she couldn't help that but she damned well didn't have to let him lure her into a verbal sparring match.

"I'll ask you once more, your highness. What do you want?"

"Ask me in and I'll tell you."

"I have no intention of asking you in. Tell me why you're here or don't. It's your choice, just as it will be my choice to shut the door in your face."

He laughed. It infuriated her but she could hardly blame him. He was tall—six two, six three—and though he stood with one shoulder leaning against the door frame, hands tucked casually into the pockets of the jacket, his pose was deceptive. He was strong, with the leanly muscled body of a well-trained athlete.

She remembered his body with painful clarity. The

feel of him under her hands. The power of him moving over her. The taste of him on her tongue.

Suddenly, he straightened, his laughter gone. "I have not come this distance to stand in your doorway," he said coldly, "and I am not going to leave until I am ready to do so. I suggest you stand aside and stop behaving like a petulant child."

A petulant child? Was that what he thought? This man who had spent hours making love to her and had then accused her of—of trading her body for profit?

Except it had not been love, it had been sex. And the sooner she got rid of him, the better.

She let go of the doorknob and stepped aside. "You have five minutes."

He strolled past her, bringing cold air and the scent of the night with him. She swung toward him, arms folded. He reached past her, pushed the door closed, then folded his arms, too. She wanted to open the door again but she'd be damned if she was going to get into a who's-in-charge-here argument with him. She was in charge, and he would surely see a tussle over the ground rules as a sign of weakness.

Instead, she looked past him at the big clock above her work table.

"Ten seconds gone," she said briskly. "You're wasting time, your highness."

"What I have to say will take longer than five minutes."

"Then you'll just have to learn to economize. More than five minutes, I'll call the police."

Instantly, his hand was wrapped around her wrist. He tugged her toward him, his dark-chocolate eyes almost black with anger.

"You do that and I'll tell every tabloid shark I can contact about how Maria Santos tried to buy a five-hundred-thousand-dollar commission by seducing a prince." He smiled thinly. "They'll lap it up."

* * * * *

What will it take for this billionaire prince to realize
he's falling in love with his mistress…?
Look for
BILLIONAIRE PRINCE, PREGNANT MISTRESS
by Sandra Marton
Available July 2009
from Harlequin Presents®.

REQUEST YOUR FREE BOOKS!

2 FREE NOVELS PLUS 2 FREE GIFTS!

Silhouette® Romantic SUSPENSE

Sparked by Danger, Fueled by Passion!

YES! Please send me 2 FREE Silhouette® Romantic Suspense novels and my 2 FREE gifts (gifts are worth about $10). After receiving them, if I don't wish to receive any more books, I can return the shipping statement marked "cancel." If I don't cancel, I will receive 4 brand-new novels every month and be billed just $4.24 per book in the U.S. or $4.99 per book in Canada. That's a savings of at least 15% off the cover price! It's quite a bargain! Shipping and handling is just 50¢ per book*. I understand that accepting the 2 free books and gifts places me under no obligation to buy anything. I can always return a shipment and cancel at any time. Even if I never buy another book from Silhouette, the two free books and gifts are mine to keep forever.

240 SDN EYL4 340 SDN EYMG

Name _____ (PLEASE PRINT)

Address _____ Apt. #

City _____ State/Prov. _____ Zip/Postal Code

Signature (if under 18, a parent or guardian must sign)

Mail to the Silhouette Reader Service:
IN U.S.A.: P.O. Box 1867, Buffalo, NY 14240-1867
IN CANADA: P.O. Box 609, Fort Erie, Ontario L2A 5X3

Not valid to current subscribers of Silhouette Romantic Suspense books.

Want to try two free books from another line?
Call 1-800-873-8635 or visit www.morefreebooks.com.

* Terms and prices subject to change without notice. Prices do not include applicable taxes. Sales tax applicable in N.Y. Canadian residents will be charged applicable provincial taxes and GST. Offer not valid in Quebec. This offer is limited to one order per household. All orders subject to approval. Credit or debit balances in a customer's account(s) may be offset by any other outstanding balance owed by or to the customer. Please allow 4 to 6 weeks for delivery. Offer available while quantities last.

Your Privacy: Silhouette is committed to protecting your privacy. Our Privacy Policy is available online at www.eHarlequin.com or upon request from the Reader Service. From time to time we make our lists of customers available to reputable third parties who may have a product or service of interest to you. If you would prefer we not share your name and address, please check here. ☐

SRS09R

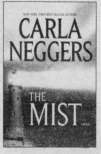

Do you crave dark and sensual paranormal tales?

Get your fix with Silhouette Nocturne!

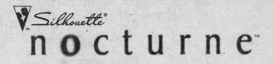

THE BELLES OF TEXAS

They're as strong as the state that raised
them. The Belle sisters aren't afraid to go
after what they want, whether it's reclaiming
their ranch or their family.

Linda Warren
CAITLYN'S PRIZE

Thanks to her deceased father's gambling
debts, Caitlyn Belle's beloved High Five Ranch
is in dire straits. Particularly because the
will stipulates that if the ranch doesn't turn
a profit in six months, it must be sold to
Judd Calhoun—the man Caitlyn jilted
fourteen years ago. And Cait knows Judd has
been waiting a long time for his revenge....

*Look for the first book
in The Belles of Texas miniseries,
on sale in July wherever books are sold.*

Silhouette®

Romantic

SUSPENSE

COMING NEXT MONTH

Available June 30, 2009

#1567 THE UNEXPECTED HERO—Rachel Lee
Conard County: The Next Generation
Newly returned from nursing in V.A. hospitals, Kristin Tate clashes
with Dr. David Marcus on her first shift at Community Hospital. Yet
clearly there's an attraction beneath the surface. And when two patients
mysteriously die on her shift, rag dolls left as a killer's signature, David is
determined to prove Kristin's innocence…or die trying.

#1568 PRINCE CHARMING FOR 1 NIGHT—Nina Bruhns
Love in 60 Seconds
To secure the return of his family's recently stolen diamond ring,
Conner Rothchild must use exotic dancer Vera Mancuso as bait for the real
thief—and not let her out of his sight. During their crash course on social
graces, he finds himself wanting her, and the feeling is mutual. But when a
cold-blooded killer kidnaps Vera, can Conner save her?

#1569 TERMS OF ATTRACTION—Kylie Brant
Alpha Squad
Blackmailed into joining a foreign president's security detail, Ava Carter
finds herself at odds with protection specialist Cael McCabe. Quickly onto
her duplicity, Cael still can't resist the heat that sizzles between them as
they track down a kidnapper deep in the South American jungles. But the
biggest risk of all will be trusting each other with their hearts.

#1570 MEDUSA'S MASTER—Cindy Dees
H.O.T. Watch
Someone is stealing priceless art from Caribbean mansions, and Special
Forces soldiers Katrina Kim and Jeff Steiger must find out who it is.
Sparks fly immediately, but as Kat comes face-to-face with the thief, they
discover an even bigger threat. With Kat now in the line of fire, can Jeff
live with the risks she takes in her work and find a way to love all of her?